Wrong Wedding Right Guy

"My first karaoke trophy," Ella said. "I'll have to clear a spot on the mantel."

"Right next to your Grammy?" he teased.

"Exactly." She hugged the trophy to her chest.

"Consider it a souvenir of your first trip to Bluestem," he said. "Something to remember us by when you're back in Lincoln."

The way he said "us" made her heart flutter. She met his gaze, her smile softening.

"I don't think I'll need a trophy to remember tonight."

His throat bobbed with a swallow. "No?"

"No." She turned the trophy slightly so its painted gold caught the light. "Some memories just stick with you."

BOOK 1

Wrong Wedding Right Guy

JoAnn Charles

Prairieland Press

Text Copyright © 2025 JoAnn Charles

All rights reserved. No part of this publication
may be reproduced, stored in a retrieval system,
or transmitted in any form or by any means
(electronic, mechanical, photocopying, recording, or any other)
except for brief quotations in printed reviews,
without the prior permission of the publisher.

The story, all names, characters, and incidents
portrayed in this work of art are fictitious.
No identification with actual persons
(living or deceased), places, buildings, and products
is intended or should be inferred.

Prairieland Press
PO Box 2404
Fremont, NE 68026-2404
Printed in the U.S.A.

Cover Design by Prairieland Press
Book Design by Prairieland Press

eBook ISBN-13: 978-1-944132-51-4
Paperback ISBN-13: 978-1-944132-50-7
Hardcover ISBN-13: 978-1-944132-52-1

*For Larry, who always supports my dreams,
and for Mom and Dad, Always!*

One

ELLA ROSE

Ella Rose steered her Honda Civic down Bluestem's Main Street, windows cracked to let in the summer air. She'd seen photos online when she'd booked her room at the Whitemore Hotel, but they hadn't quite captured the town's simple charm: brick streets, flower boxes brimming with color, hand-painted signs above tidy storefronts.

She pulled into the small parking lot of the Whitemore, cut the engine, and just sat for a moment, admiring the obvious care someone had lavished on the old two-story brick hotel.

The garden that lined the walkway was a riot of color, and the air was thick with the scent of petunias and some other flowers she couldn't name. Laughter drifted through an open window. Wind chimes tinkled softly on the porch.

Inside, the lobby was a blend of old-world charm and modern comfort, with its gleaming hardwood floor and pressed tin ceiling. The air smelled of coffee and freshly baked goodies. To her right, wingback chairs flanked a fireplace with an ornate mantel adorned with fresh wildflowers. An antique desk served as the check-in counter, brass keys gleaming in orderly rows behind it.

Ella Rose set her overnight bag and guitar case down with a sigh of relief and rang the bell on the counter.

"Be right there!" called a voice from the back.

A woman appeared, petite and smiling, with auburn hair pulled back in a no-nonsense ponytail, balancing a plate of chocolate chip cookies. She offered one with a smile, then set the plate on the counter. "Welcome to the Whitemore! I'm LeAnne Hudson. How can I help you?"

"I have a reservation—Ella Tate," she replied, using the name she always listed for work. Years of singing at weddings had taught her to keep things simple and professional.

LeAnne scanned the computer, fingers quick and practiced. "There you are. Arriving today, leaving Sunday. You're in the Jeri Southern room. She was a jazz singer from Royal, Nebraska. Did you know that when you booked?"

"I did," Ella Rose said, smiling. "My dad is a big fan."

"Wonderful view of the rose garden from that room," LeAnne said, sliding a registration card and pen across the polished desk. "What brings you to Bluestem?"

Ella Rose hesitated. She could say she was in town to sing at a wedding—that was the truth—but she'd come a day early for a reason. A little solitude before the usual performance-day scramble. "I'm here for work and a bit of rest," she said, keeping her tone light. "Just a quick weekend trip."

LeAnne accepted that with a nod. "Well, we're happy to have you."

Ella Rose signed her name and returned the card.

"Have you eaten supper yet?" LeAnne asked. "We only serve breakfast here, but the Rusty Spur has a wonderful grilled chicken salad. Plus their Rusty burger and fries are legendary in this part of Nebraska."

Ella Rose's stomach rumbled in reply. "Thank you. I'll probably head over after I get settled."

"Room 7 is up the stairs, end of the hall, to the right." LeAnne slid over a big brass key and a small card. "Breakfast is from seven to nine. WiFi password is on the card, along with my cell number, in case you need anything—night or day."

The Jeri Southern room was even better than the website had promised. A queen-sized four-poster bed took up most of the space, dressed in a deep navy comforter that made her think of a midnight jazz club—smoky, secret, and a little glamorous.

A vintage phonograph sat perched on a cabinet, flanked by a trio of Southern's albums. Velvet curtains framed a view of the rose garden, and a tufted armchair practically begged her to curl up with a book. Even the bathroom, with all its retro tile and modern fixtures, felt like an invitation to relax and unwind, and not an afterthought.

Ella Rose hung her dress in the wardrobe,

checked it for wrinkles, and set her guitar gently on the bed. Unpacking her toiletries, she randomly hummed the half-written melody that had been haunting her since spring. The chorus felt right, but the verses still needed work.

She splashed water on her face, freshened her lipstick, and headed back downstairs, letting herself savor the quiet of the empty lobby. Stained glass above the front door cast a mosaic of light across the wood floor.

Drawn toward an archway to the left of the grand staircase, Ella Rose found herself in a room that appeared to be an old-fashioned parlor.

This room clearly served as the heart of the old hotel. Larger than the lobby sitting area, it featured several seating arrangements: sofas around a coffee table, a cushioned window seat, and a game table in one corner. A grand piano stood in another corner, its dark wood gleaming despite its age. Bookshelves lined one wall, filled with classics, local history books, and board games.

Ella Rose stepped into the room and let out a small, contented sigh. This wasn't the cold, impersonal neatness of the chain hotels she usually found herself in. Here, every scuff on the floor and furniture seemed to tell a story. It was a place with roots, with character.

A man sat on one sofa, newspaper in hand, sleeves rolled up to reveal tanned forearms. He looked so at ease, Ella Rose hesitated, not wanting to intrude. But before she could back out, her phone rang, shattering the quiet. The man's head snapped up, startled, as she fumbled to answer.

"Rosie, here," she said, cheeks flushing at her own clumsiness.

"Just checking to make sure you're all set for tomorrow," her boss's voice barked in her ear. No pleasantries, just the business at hand.

"Yes. I have the list of songs they requested on my phone." She pressed the phone close, aware of every word echoing in the near-silence. "This place is amazing. You should see it."

"Fantastic. I can't wait to hear all about it when you get home. Call me if you need anything. Good luck at the wedding tomorrow."

The line went dead before she could respond. Typical Dave. Ella Rose tucked her phone away and risked a look at the stranger. He met her gaze, eyes quietly amused.

"Sorry," she said, letting a rueful smile show. "I didn't mean to disturb you. I'm just exploring."

The man lowered his paper, his smile broadening into something that transformed his already handsome features into something truly striking. He had the kind of face that seemed designed to smile, deep creases forming around warm brown eyes that crinkled at the corners.

"Not disturbing me at all," he said. "I'm just taking a breather. Plenty of room to share, if you'd like." He gestured casually toward the armchair across from him.

Ella Rose hesitated, then stepped fully into the parlor. Something about both the room and the stranger softened her usual professional reserve. "Thanks. I think I will. I've only just arrived and I'm exhausted."

The man folded his newspaper and set it aside.

"Long trip?" he asked.

"About five hours," Ella Rose said, sinking into the chair. "I could have been here sooner but I took the scenic route. Interstate 80 gets so monotonous."

He nodded, as if approving her choice. "Back

roads are always better. You're Rosie, right? Here for a wedding?"

She blinked, caught off guard. "Word travels fast here! I only just checked in."

He grinned, a little sheepishly. "I overheard your call. Plus, I'm here for a wedding, too. My brother's, actually. Since there's only one wedding at the Whitemore this weekend, I figured we're here for the same one."

He offered his hand. "Sawyer Jennings. Best man at my brother Caleb's wedding tomorrow."

She took it, feeling the calluses and the warmth of his grip. "Nice to meet you, Sawyer. I'm Rosie, as you know, and I'm going to sing at a wedding tomorrow. Apparently, your brother's wedding."

Sawyer laughed, the sound deep and genuine. "My brother will be glad to know the entertainment has arrived. One less thing for his bride to worry about tonight."

Ella Rose nodded sympathetically. "Weddings can turn stressful in a hurry!"

"Tell me about it! Especially when your future sister-in-law gets it in her head you need a date, and is determined to set you up with her maid of honor."

Ella Rose winced. "Is that why you're hiding here with a newspaper instead of celebrating somewhere with the wedding party?"

"Absolutely!" Sawyer ran a hand through his hair, which looked like it was used to being ruffled. "But enough about me. How does someone become Rosie, the wedding singer?"

Ella Rose laughed. "My family is musical. My granddad played banjo and guitar in a bluegrass band, my dad's a jazz pianist, and my mom sings alto. It was inescapable."

She gestured toward the ceiling. "I have a guitar upstairs that was my grandfather's. He gave it to me when I started writing my own songs."

"You write music, too?" Sawyer leaned forward.

Ella Rose nodded, feeling that familiar mixture of pride and vulnerability.

"I'd love to hear one of your songs sometime," Sawyer said, the sincerity in his voice making Ella Rose's cheeks warm slightly.

"Maybe," she replied, surprised to find she meant it. She rarely shared her original music with anyone. "Your turn. What's your story, Sawyer Jennings?"

"Much less interesting," Sawyer said with a wry smile. "Born and raised about fifteen minutes from here. Went away to college. Tried out corporate life in Omaha—banks, neckties, all of it. Hated every second."

"So what do you love?" Ella Rose asked.

Sawyer didn't hesitate. "Landscaping. Growing things, getting the dirt under my nails all day. I own a small design company now." He gave a little shrug, as if to apologize for how simple it sounded.

A sudden, unmistakable growl interrupted them. Sawyer's eyebrows shot up. "Was that an actual stomach growl, or did I miss spotting a small wolf in here?" he teased, scanning the room in mock alarm.

Ella Rose pressed a hand to her middle, laughing. "Sorry! I skipped lunch to get on the road, and I'm paying for it now."

"When was the last time you ate?" Sawyer's tone was all concern.

"Around eight this morning," she said. "Coffee and a muffin."

"That's not breakfast. That's survival rations," Sawyer said. "No wonder your stomach is angry. It's almost six."

His concern made Ella Rose smile. "I was planning to grab dinner after getting settled. The innkeeper recommended a place called the Rusty Spur."

"LeAnne has excellent taste," Sawyer said. "The Rusty Spur has the best burgers in three counties. And the fries! They give you so many, they have to serve them in a separate basket!"

He hesitated, then said, "I was just about to walk down there for supper myself. Would you like to join me?"

Ella Rose felt a flicker of surprise, followed by a pleasant warmth. She rarely socialized while working, preferring to keep things professional. But Sawyer wasn't her client; his future sister-in-law was. And there was something about his straightforward manner that made dinner with him seem more like a treat than a risk.

Still, caution made her pause. "I wouldn't want to take you away from your best man duties. Aren't you supposed to be at a rehearsal dinner or something?"

Sawyer laughed, the sound rich and full. "Trust me, no one is going to miss me at that dinner, including the maid of honor. After three days of wedding chaos, I think I've earned a meal with someone who isn't obsessed with seating charts or flower arrangements." His voice softened. "No pressure, though. If you want a quiet night in before tomorrow, I get it."

His consideration sealed it for Ella Rose. "Company sounds nice," she said, and stood. Sawyer unfolded himself from the sofa, and she realized just how tall he was—at least eight inches taller than her.

Sawyer nodded for her to go first, and together they stepped out onto the porch. The heat had mellowed, settling into a golden warmth that softened the edges of the evening. Ella Rose breathed it in, letting herself enjoy the unfamiliar quiet of a new town with nothing on her schedule but supper with a friend.

Sawyer fell into step beside her, hands tucked in his pockets, matching her pace as they set off down the sidewalk. "What kind of music do you usually sing?" Sawyer asked.

"For weddings, it depends on the couple. Everything from classical to country to pop. For my own songs, I'm drawn to country and folk music. Songs that tell a story about the quiet moments that make up our everyday lives."

They turned onto Main Street. The Rusty

Spur's wooden sign creaked in the breeze. Laughter and conversation spilled from the open doorway, mingling with the smell of grilled burgers and french fries.

As they reached the entrance, Sawyer's hand brushed the small of her back; a brief, respectful touch that sent a pleasant shiver through her.

Inside, the place was alive with Friday night energy, but Ella Rose felt oddly calm. Maybe it was Sawyer, or the town, or the simple act of being somewhere new. But inside Ella Rose, a melody was taking shape.

Not a love song. Not yet. But maybe, just maybe, the beginning of one.

Two

SAWYER

Sawyer pushed open the door of the Rusty Spur and held it for Rosie, catching a hint of her perfume as she passed, a rose floral scent that seemed made for her. It had been a long time since he'd brought a woman here, or anywhere, really. Two years, maybe more, since he'd even tried to make room in his life for dating. Not since he'd left Omaha for Bluestem.

"Welcome to Bluestem's finest bar and grill," he said, gesturing as they stepped inside. "And by finest, I mean Bluestem's only bar and grill."

He watched as she took in the worn wooden tables, vintage beer signs, and the collection of license plates covering one wall. Classic country played from the corner speakers, just loud enough to be appreciated, but not so loud that folks couldn't talk. He was both curious about her opinion of the bar and surprised by his longing for her to like it.

"It's perfect," Rosie said, and the way she said it, soft and certain, made him believe she meant it.

Sawyer scanned the room and spotted an empty booth tucked away in the corner. "How about over there?" he asked, pointing. Rosie nodded, and they wove their way through the maze of tables, earning a few curious glances from the regulars.

The wooden benches squeaked as they slid into the booth. A tinny rendition of a Johnny Cash classic hummed in the background, providing a comfortable backdrop to their conversation.

Sawyer flipped open a menu and leaned across the table, dropping his voice as if he were about to share a secret. "My personal rule: always go for the most deep-fried item on the menu."

Rosie tapped her chin, a sly twitch in her smile. "So that would be…"

Sawyer flashed a grin. "Fried chicken strips

with fried cauliflower, fried onions, and fried mushrooms," he said, ticking each one off on his fingers.

She shook her head, laughing. "I think I'll stick with the grilled chicken salad, thanks."

Just then, an older woman approached the table, balancing two glasses of water and a bowl of lemon wedges. Her eyebrows shot up when she spotted Sawyer. "Sawyer Jennings, aren't you supposed to be at the Whitemore, helping Caleb get ready for that big fancy wedding?"

"Hello to you, too, Mrs. K," Sawyer said, grinning up at her. "The rumor going around town is you're serving peach cobbler today. So frankly, Mrs. K., how was I supposed to stay away?" he asked, rubbing his hands together in anticipation.

The woman shook her head at Sawyer's comment. Her expression was a mixture of mock skepticism and amusement, as if she were trying to decide whether to scold him for neglecting his duties or praise him for his impeccable taste in dessert.

Sawyer nodded toward Rosie before the older woman could say any more. "Mrs. K., this is Rosie. She's in town for the wedding."

Mrs. K.'s demeanor softened instantly. "Welcome to Bluestem, Rosie. Glad to have you."

He looked over at Rosie and smiled. "And this wonderful woman, Rosie, is Mrs. K. She was Bluestem's third grade teacher for thirty years, until she retired to help her son and her husband run this little bar and grill."

"Speaking of which, I better get back to doing my job, or my bosses might fire me!" She laughed at her own joke and opened up her notepad. "What'll it be, Hon?"

Rosie set her menu down. "Grilled chicken salad and a glass of white wine, please."

"And I'll take the Rusty burger, with bacon and extra pickles, fries on the side, and a beer," Sawyer said.

Rosie raised her eyebrows in mock surprise. "Didn't you just say the rule is to always order the most deep-fried thing on the menu?"

Sawyer feigned a look of deep contemplation. "I did say that. I guess I'm a rule breaker."

Mrs. K. nodded her head. "Now that's a true statement, if ever I heard one. During his time in my class, Sawyer never met a rule he wouldn't break."

Sawyer gave Mrs. K. a pleading look. "Don't

go telling all my secrets, Mrs. K. I'm trying to impress the girl, here."

Rosie laughed, and Sawyer felt a warmth spread through him, as satisfying as any cold beer.

Mrs. K. lowered her voice. "You're doing just fine, Sawyer." She winked at Rosie, scribbled down their order, and disappeared toward the kitchen.

Sawyer reached for a lemon wedge, giving it a gentle squeeze into his water. The restaurant chatter faded into the background. "So, wedding singer," he said, settling back, "you must have some stories."

"Oh, I've got stories," Rosie said. "I think one of my favorites is when the bride walked down the aisle to 'Oops!... I Did It Again.'"

Sawyer nearly choked. "You're kidding!"

"Nope! She said it was *their* song."

He grinned, imagining the scene, right as Mrs. K. slid their plates onto the table. Rosie's salad looked fresh and colorful, but Sawyer caught her eyeing his mountainous basket of fries.

"Time to let you in on a local secret. No one in Bluestem is ever allowed to eat a whole order of Rusty Spur fries by themselves. I'm forced to share." He slid the basket to the middle of the table.

She raised an eyebrow. "Is that so? I don't remember seeing that rule posted anywhere."

"It's unwritten. Very exclusive knowledge. Only true Bluestem locals know about it."

"In that case…" She leaned in, and Sawyer noticed the gold flecks in her eyes. She plucked a fry from the basket. "Guess I have no choice but to help you out. You're already breaking one rule by not ordering the most deep-fried thing. I wouldn't want you to break two rules in the space of half an hour."

She tasted the fry, her expression turning from playful to honestly impressed. "Wow! I might have to move here just for these."

He smiled at that. He could imagine her here, a regular at the Rusty Spur, maybe even writing songs about the locals and their small-town quirks. His mind wandered to the idea of sharing more than just fries with her—a few more meals, a few more days.

As they ate, Rosie continued to share wedding stories: the bride who accidentally set her veil on fire with a unity candle, the ring bearer who fell asleep and snored loudly through the vows, the curious deer who photobombed a couple's out-door wedding portrait.

Sawyer laughed more than he had in months. She had a way of spinning chaos into comedy that he found utterly charming.

Not for the first time, he wondered if she was single. She hadn't mentioned anyone, and she'd agreed to supper with him. Of course, there was that phone call she'd gotten, just as she walked into the parlor...

"So," Rosie said, crossing her arms on the table, "what's the deal with you and the maid of honor?"

Sawyer groaned. "Amber, my soon-to-be sister-in-law, has it in her head that no one should show up to her wedding single. Lindsey's her friend from college. She's been trying to set us up for weeks."

"And you're not interested?" Rosie tilted her head, a strand of hair falling across her cheek.

"It's the principle of the thing. Being paired up like—" He paused, searching for the right image.

"Noah's Ark?" Rosie asked.

"Exactly! Two by two, nice and tidy."

Rosie nodded, tracing the condensation on her water glass. "So what's your strategy? Hide in the coat closet during the reception?"

"I thought about it, but it seems undignified. I might just come down with a sudden, highly contagious illness."

"A classic move." Rosie's eyes danced with humor. "Very effective. But you might miss out on cake."

"You're right," Sawyer said. "And I do love cake. Looks like I need professional advice here."

Rosie took a sip of her wine and stared at him over the rim of her glass. "In my extensive wedding experience, you have three options. One, bring a date, real or fake, as a buffer."

"It's a little late for that, unless…" Sawyer let the suggestion hang playfully in the air between them, his heart beating a little faster at the thought of Rosie attending the wedding as his date.

Rosie's cheeks colored slightly, but she continued as if she hadn't noticed the implication. "Option two: keep so busy with wedding tasks you're never in one place long enough for the setup to work."

"Promising. What's the third option?"

"Be honest. Tell your sister-in-law you appreciate her concern, but you'd rather meet people on your own terms."

Sawyer wrinkled his nose. "That sounds suspiciously like healthy communication."

"I know. Terrible idea, right?" Rosie grinned and helped herself to another fry.

Sawyer took the last bite of his burger, chewing slowly. "Do you ever get tired of weddings?" he asked. "Or does it still feel special, even after the hundredth 'I do'?"

Rosie paused, her fork hovering over her salad. "I still love it," she said, her voice sincere. "There's something magical about the beginning of forever. Even when an Elvis impersonator performs the ceremony."

Sawyer watched her in the soft restaurant light, noticing the way she blushed at her own sentimentality. "You have a romantic streak," he said.

Her cheeks colored faintly. "Maybe a little."

"If you ever need a plus-one for an Elvis wedding, I'm your guy," he said, only half-joking.

She laughed again. "I'll keep that in mind."

Sawyer took another fry, mostly to keep his

hands from reaching out to her. She wasn't flashy, but she sparkled in her own quiet way. A little offbeat. A little unpredictable.

And, if he wasn't careful, totally unforgettable.

Three

ELLA ROSE

The clatter of metal against wood caught Ella Rose's attention. In the far corner, Wyatt, the owner, was battling a tangle of cords as he set up a battered karaoke machine and its microphone stand. A few regulars watched with grins; others groaned playfully as they nursed their drinks. Ella Rose glanced at Sawyer, catching the flicker of a smile pulling at his lips.

"Karaoke night?" she asked, swirling the wine in her glass.

"Every Friday since Wyatt and his dad bought the place. Four years running."

She nudged his foot under the table. "So, are you planning to serenade me?"

He let out an easy laugh. "Not a chance. But

I'd bet a whole dollar, you have nothing to fear from a little karaoke."

"That depends entirely on the song," she said. She tucked a stray lock of hair behind her ear.

"Mind if I sit next to you?" Sawyer asked, already sliding out of his seat and motioning for her to scoot over. "The view is better from your side."

Warmth bloomed in her cheeks as he settled in beside her. Sawyer draped his arm along the back of the booth, casual but close. "Much better. Now I won't miss a thing," he said.

The speakers crackled to life, and Wyatt's voice boomed out. "All right, folks! Friday Night Rusty Mic at the Spur is officially underway! Sign-up's at the bar. Tonight's winner takes home—" Wyatt fumbled beneath the counter and produced a garish gold microphone trophy, "—the legendary Rusty Mic." Whistles and hollers erupted from every corner of the bar.

Ella Rose arched an eyebrow. "The legendary Rusty Mic?"

Sawyer leaned in, his hand settling gently on her shoulder to draw her a fraction closer. "Don't let the name fool you. It's actually a kid's plastic microphone spray-painted gold and glued to a wood block. But around here, it's as good as a Grammy."

Ella Rose laughed. "Impressive. Very prestigious."

"Oh, absolutely," Sawyer said, straight-faced. "Competition's brutal."

People were already lining up by the bar, clutching song slips or thumbing through the battered karaoke binders. A woman in bedazzled denim, at least sixty and proud of it, stepped up to the edge of the stage.

"That's Irene," Sawyer said, following her gaze. "Town librarian. She does a Dolly Parton tune every Friday without fail."

As if on cue, the twangy opening of "Jolene" filled the bar. Irene took the stage, moving with the confidence of someone who'd sung the song a hundred times before, and maybe she had. Her voice pulsed with personality, and when she finished, the place erupted in applause.

Next up, a young couple tackled a Jason Aldean and Kelly Clarkson duet. Their enthusiasm far outweighed their vocal skill, but the crowd cheered them on, anyway.

Three more performances followed: a

teenage girl with a surprisingly powerful voice, an elderly man who forgot half the words but won everyone over with his grin, and a group of women who performed a lively, choreographed routine to "Man! I Feel Like a Woman!"

When Wyatt returned to the stage, he scanned the crowd. "All right, who's next? Don't be shy—we're just getting warmed up!"

Sawyer leaned in, voice pitched low so only she could hear. "You should sign up."

Ella Rose shook her head. "I'm just here to enjoy the show."

Sawyer grinned, an easy, coaxing smile that threatened to unravel her resistance completely. "Come on, Rosie. When's the last time you sang just for fun? Not for a wedding, not for a gig—just for you?"

Somewhere in his words she heard a dare, or maybe an invitation. He had a point. It had been a long time—longer than she cared to admit—since she'd sung anything just for the joy of it. "You're persistent, you know that?"

"I prefer supportive."

She laughed, then surrendered. "If I embarrass myself, I'm blaming you."

He lifted his glass in salute. "Deal."

Ella Rose slipped from the booth, acutely aware of his eyes on her as she strode to the bar. She signed her name, scanned the songbook, and scribbled down her choice.

"Next up, Rosie singing the Patsy Cline classic, 'Crazy'!" Wyatt said. "Let's give her a big hand!"

A nervous flutter swept through Ella Rose as she climbed the steps to the stage. But the nerves faded as soon as she wrapped her hands around the microphone.

As the familiar chords filled the air, Ella Rose took a deep breath and let herself sink into the music. Her voice rang out, clear and pure. The chatter faded; phones disappeared. Every eye in the Spur landed on her. She stole a glance at Sawyer; he watched, open admiration etched on his face. When she winked at him between lines, he gave her a goofy thumbs-up that nearly made her laugh mid-verse.

Ella Rose closed her eyes, losing herself in the music, pouring her heart into the song. By the final chorus, she sang not for the crowd, not even for Sawyer, but for the love of singing itself. When the last note faded, the room exploded. Some people got to their feet. Ella Rose felt her whole body hum with the kind of joy she'd forgotten was possible.

She took a quick bow, adrenaline buzzing through her, and made her way to the bar for a word with Wyatt. The applause and cheers continued to echo around her as she headed back to Sawyer's table. All around, strangers stopped her to shake hands, pat her on the back, or shout compliments across the room.

"That was flat-out incredible," Sawyer said, standing as she approached. He wrapped her in a brief, congratulatory hug that, for a split second, left her feet dangling above the floor. "Seriously, Rosie. You have the voice of an angel."

She blushed as he set her down. "Thank you. I forgot how much fun that could be." She glanced up at him, her voice softer. "Thank you for talking me into it."

After two more songs, Wyatt hopped back onto the stage. "Folks, I've got a special surprise for you all. Rosie registered two songs for tonight—and this time, she's bringing a partner! Give it up for our own Sawyer Jennings, everyone!"

Sawyer's eyes went wide, his jaw dropping in mock horror as he turned to Ella Rose. "Traitor," he hissed in her ear.

Ella Rose tried—unsuccessfully—to hide her laughter behind her hand. "Must be your supportive spirit rubbing off on me."

Sawyer let out a long, theatrical sigh. "Fine. But if I end up on YouTube, I'm blaming you."

She flashed him a wicked grin. "Relax. It'll only go viral if you mess up spectacularly."

Sawyer ran a hand through his hair with an exaggerated groan. "You're really not inspiring confidence here."

He stood, offering her his hand. "Let's get this over with."

She took it, her fingers curling into his. "Lead the way."

"What are we singing?" Sawyer whispered as they reached the stage.

"'Jackson,'" she said. "You'll be great. Just grumble and growl like Johnny Cash. The rest will take care of itself."

Wyatt handed them each a mic and clapped Sawyer on the back. "Never thought I'd see this day, Jennings!" he said, his voice booming through the speakers. "This is gonna be epic, folks."

The crowd cheered with anticipation. Sawyer stared at Ella Rose as the first notes played, and she gave him an encouraging nod. "Ready?" she asked, her voice just for him.

"Ready as I'll ever be," he said, his voice filled with mock trepidation.

Ella Rose took the opening, her voice sharp and playful. Then it was Sawyer's turn, and, after a shaky start, he found his footing, the rough edge of his voice surprisingly perfect for the song. Their voices mingled in the chorus, and Ella Rose felt a jolt of delight at how well it worked.

It was easy; the way singing with her family had always been easy. She tossed her hair, playing up the part, and Sawyer, growing bolder, waved his western hat and fired off his lines with comic flair.

They leaned into the banter, faces close, nearly nose to nose. Ella Rose laughed so hard at one of Sawyer's exaggerated eyebrow wiggles she had to turn away from the mic. He grinned, clearly pleased to have cracked her up.

Their laughter bled into the performance, and even the mistakes—Sawyer missing a beat, Ella Rose jumping in too soon—just made it better. By the last chorus, the whole bar was singing along. When they finished, the Rusty Spur erupted in applause.

Sawyer spun Ella Rose under his arm before they both bowed. The crowd roared, and Sawyer lifted their joined hands in victory.

Wyatt bounded onto the stage, clapping. "I'm calling it early—best duet we've had in ages! The Rusty Mic goes to Rosie and Sawyer!"

The crowd cheered as Ella Rose accepted the trophy. It was, indeed, just a gold-painted plastic microphone perched atop a wooden base. The gaudy trophy was both ridiculous and oddly sentimental.

"Speech!" someone called, and the chant caught on.

Ella Rose looked at Sawyer, arching one eyebrow in challenge. He groaned, but took the mic. "I'd like to thank my shower for being my only audience until tonight," he said, drawing laughter. "And Rosie, for getting me up here. But mostly, thanks to everyone at the Spur for making her first night in Bluestem a good one."

Compliments and handshakes interrupted their exit from the stage, and a dozen people stopped them on their way back to the booth.

"That wasn't so bad, was it?" Ella Rose asked as they slid back into their seats.

"It was terrible," he said, though the teasing light in his eyes gave him away. "But also... kind of great!"

Ella Rose set the trophy on the table, the gold paint already flaking. She couldn't help smiling at it.

"You keep it," Sawyer said. "You're the real talent here."

Ella Rose traced the edge of the wooden base. "My first karaoke trophy. I'll have to clear a spot on the mantel."

"Right next to your Grammy?" he teased.

"Exactly." She hugged the trophy to her chest.

"Consider it a souvenir of your first trip to Bluestem," he said. "Something to remember us by when you're back in Lincoln."

The way he said "us" made her heart flutter. She met his gaze, her smile softening. "I don't think I'll need a trophy to remember tonight."

His throat bobbed with a swallow. "No?"

"No." She turned the trophy slightly so its painted gold caught the light. "Some memories just stick with you."

Sawyer didn't say anything. He just looked at her, really looked at her, like he was memorizing the way she looked right now. When he finally spoke, his voice was gentle. "It's late. We should probably head back to the hotel. Big day tomorrow."

Ella Rose nodded and rose to her feet, cradling the trophy like a prized possession before tucking it safely away in her purse. As they wove through the crowded bar, she hoped Sawyer would reach for her hand again.

She shook the thought away and reminded herself that she barely knew this man. But it didn't matter. She wanted to know him, wanted to know all about him. That realization was both thrilling and unsettling. Because this wasn't just a night to remember. It was quickly becoming the one night she knew she'd never forget.

Four

SAWYER

Sawyer held the door for Rosie and followed her out into the night, pulling it shut behind them. The silence was a relief after the noise of the crowd, which still echoed in his head.

Rosie tilted her head back with a soft gasp.

Sawyer followed her gaze. Stars. Thousands of them. He'd seen them a hundred times, but standing there beside her, they seemed strange and beautiful, as if he were seeing them for the very first time.

"The perk of living in the middle of nowhere," he said. "No city lights getting in the way."

"They're incredible," Rosie whispered. Her words hung in the air, reverent and soft, as if speaking too loudly might shatter the delicate beauty above them. "In Lincoln, we're lucky to spot the Big Dipper. This is... it's like someone spilled glitter across black velvet."

Sawyer looked at her, the starlight catching on her features, her eyes wide with wonder. "That's a songwriter's description if I've ever heard one. You should write that down."

She nodded. "I should."

A cool breeze ruffled the leaves and tugged at the loose ends of her hair. Rosie shivered, rubbing her arms. Sawyer didn't think twice. He shrugged out of his worn leather jacket and offered it to her.

Rosie hesitated, her gaze flicking from the jacket to him, a playful smile touching her lips. "You sure? It might clash with my ensemble."

He laughed. "I think you can pull it off."

He draped the jacket over her shoulders, careful not to brush too close, though the urge to do so was strong. Together, they started down the sidewalk, past shuttered shops and empty benches. The street lamps cast soft halos that flickered as they passed beneath each one.

Sawyer watched her out of the corner of his eye as she took everything in: the buildings, the breeze, the stars. And he realized he was more captivated by her than by the surrounding view. The way she tilted her head when she was curious. The way she seemed to glow when she was happy.

They turned onto the tree-lined side street that led to the Whitemore Hotel. Moonlight filtered through the branches, painting the sidewalk in silver patterns. Rosie's arm brushed his when she stepped around a crack in the pavement, and her perfume mingled with the scent of flowers and summer air.

When her fingers touched his, Sawyer thought it might have been by accident. But her hand stayed there, close—waiting. He laced his fingers with hers, slowly, giving her the chance to pull away.

She didn't.

"Is this okay?" he asked, his voice low.

Rosie squeezed his hand, her answer soft but certain. "More than okay."

They walked that way the rest of the block, steps in rhythm, hands joined. Sawyer paid attention to everything—the rhythm of their steps in unison, the distant hoot of an owl, the irregular beat of his heart.

All too soon, the Whitemore Hotel appeared at the end of the block, its windows glowing softly. Sawyer slowed, wishing the walk could last a little longer.

They crossed the threshold into the lobby, their footsteps echoing against the wooden floor. Rosie paused at the foot of the grand staircase, her hand still in his, neither of them quite ready to say goodnight.

"I have this pre-wedding groomsman thing tomorrow at eleven. But if you're free in the morning, maybe we could meet for breakfast before the madness kicks in?"

Rosie's face lit up. "I'd love that."

"I'll bring the food. I think I can steal something from the wedding brunch without too many folks noticing."

"Great. I'll bring my guitar," Rosie said.

"Nine o'clock work? We can meet in the rose garden."

She nodded. "Nine o'clock is perfect."

Sawyer let go of her hand and tucked a loose strand of hair behind her ear, his fingers lingering a moment longer than necessary.

"Thank you for tonight," he said, voice

rougher than he expected. "For the duet. The walk. The company."

Rosie smiled up at him. "Thank you for the stars."

He bent down, and his lips lightly brushed hers.

"See you in the morning," she said, her voice a soft echo of everything he was feeling.

"Count on it," he said, stepping back. He waited until she'd vanished up the stairs before he turned and headed for his truck, leather jacket slung over his arm.

He hadn't planned on taking anyone to the Rusty Spur tonight. He certainly hadn't expected to end up singing, or swapping stories, or finding himself wishing the evening could start all over again.

But as he slid behind the wheel, he glanced up, just once, at the velvet sky dusted with stars—and grinned. Tomorrow would be frantic. A day filled with interruptions.

But tonight? Tonight, he had the memory of her hand in his, the dizzying shock of her smile, and the unmistakable magic of something just beginning.

Five

ELLA ROSE

Ella Rose sat at the wrought-iron patio set in the Whitemore's rose garden, her guitar resting across her knees. The garden was alive with color—pinks, reds, and yellows tumbling over each other, dew still clinging to the velvet petals. For a moment, the only sounds were the soft strum of strings and the distant chirp of a robin.

She let her eyes drift closed, fingers picking out the new melody she'd been working on since sunrise, notes drifting up into the morning air like the story of a dream she wasn't ready to leave behind.

She replayed the memory for the hundredth time: the karaoke stage, the laughter, the star-lit walk back to the Whitemore, and that gentle, unexpected goodnight kiss that had left her smiling into her pillow. It seemed impossible that it had all happened in one night.

She checked her watch. Just after nine. The song's final note lingered, then faded, and she eased the guitar into its case, careful with the old, polished wood.

The garden gate creaked. Ella Rose looked up, pulse tripping, to see Sawyer coming down the brick path, picnic basket in hand.

"Sorry I'm late," he said, a little out of breath. "A friend from town flagged me down. Someone she knows wants a gazebo built, and she wondered if I'd be interested."

Ella Rose smothered a smile. "You're forgiven. Especially since you come bearing gifts."

Sawyer slid the basket onto the table. "Breakfast courtesy of the wedding brunch."

She eyed the basket, teasing. "I hope you brought enough for both of us."

Sawyer grinned and flicked open the lid. "Depends how hungry you are. I might have gone a little overboard."

He spread a checkered cloth over the table, then started unloading the feast: a thermos of coffee, muffins, fruit, flaky pastries. Their hands brushed as they worked, the simple contact sending a small thrill through her.

She settled beside him, shoulder brushing his. "Should we dig in?"

Sawyer handed her a plate, his smile crooked. "Absolutely. It's been, what, ten hours since your last meal? You must be starving."

"Practically fainting from hunger," she said, reaching for a blueberry muffin, the sugar sparkling in the sunlight. "This looks amazing."

It was a picnic, but a private one, and the world beyond the garden faded. Conversation bubbled up and drifted as easily as the breeze that stirred the rose bushes. Every time Ella Rose let herself glimpse Sawyer—really look at him, the way he watched her with an openness that was both startling and sweet—her heart did a funny little dance.

Sawyer picked up her guitar, turning it gently in his hands. "Your grandfather's, right?" His hands were steady, strong. Respectful.

A flicker of warmth danced through her as she nodded, watching him cradle the instrument. "He gave it to me on my fifteenth birthday," she replied. "I doubt either of us realized how much it would end up meaning to me."

Sawyer looked at her, voice soft. "He must be so proud."

Her throat tightened. She twisted her fingers together in her lap, staring at the guitar. "I think he is. But... singing at weddings was never the dream. I always figured I'd have my own songs recorded by now."

Sawyer said nothing for a second, then he set the guitar down and leaned in a little. His voice was low, measured. "What's stopping you?"

"Fear, maybe?" It was the first time she'd said it out loud. "The thought of failing at the one thing I love most?"

"Don't give up on that dream, Rosie. Ever. That voice of yours? Angelic. And I'm not just saying that because we won that beautiful gold trophy."

She laughed, surprised and touched by how much his words mattered. "Now you're just flattering me."

Sawyer shook his head. "Not even a little. Promise."

Ella Rose met his gaze. It was disarming how quickly the conversation had become personal.

She cleared her throat, shifting the spotlight off herself. "Tell me more about you," she said. "Last night, you said you worked in Omaha for awhile. Finance, right?"

Sawyer nodded, a wry smile tugging at his lips. "Yeah. When I was eighteen, I couldn't wait to get out of Bluestem. Finance seemed like the smart choice. I landed a job with a big firm right after graduation. It was exactly what I thought I wanted."

Ella Rose tilted her head. "But?"

Sawyer let out a breath, running his fingers through his hair. "But the reality was... different. I was sixteen floors up, stuck behind a desk, strangled by neckties that made my eyes water." He laughed, but there was little humor in it. "I always thought I'd love living in the city, but that office felt like—" He paused. "Like wearing shoes that pinch in all the wrong places."

Ella Rose smiled. "So you came back and started your own landscape design company."

"Biggest leap of my life. My dad still shakes his head. Says he can't believe I left a real career to, quote, 'dig in the dirt.'"

"And what do you think?"

Sawyer didn't hesitate. "I think it was the

best decision I've ever made." He paused, a playful glint in his eye. "Except for the decision to ask you to supper last night."

She felt herself blush. "I'm kind of partial to that decision myself."

They lingered over breakfast, their conversation meandering as easily as the butterflies drifting among the roses. When their plates were empty, Sawyer stood, gesturing down one of the winding paths between the rose bushes. "Want to explore the garden with me?"

Ella Rose let him help her to her feet, and they strolled side by side along the path. Every flowerbed was bursting, each rose more beautiful than the last. "This garden is so beautiful," she said, breathing in the sweet air. "I've always loved roses. Each one's a little different. I'm glad my parents named me after them." She trailed her fingers along a blossom, marveling at the delicate layers.

Sawyer reached past her to touch the same flower, his arm brushing hers. The contact was light, but it sent a shiver up her arm. "This one reminds me of you," he said.

"How so?" she asked, unable to look away from him.

"It stands out. Even in a crowd." His smile was crooked, half-shy, half-sure. "Like you."

Something inside her melted. Time seemed to slow, the air thick with sunlight and unspoken words. Then Sawyer's phone chimed, shattering the stillness.

"Duty calls?" she asked, trying to keep the disappointment from her voice.

Sawyer groaned. "It's from Caleb." He held up his phone so she could see the screen: *Have you seen my cufflinks?*

Ella Rose couldn't help but grin. "Wedding day nerves. Everything feels like a crisis."

Sawyer took his time packing up the remnants of their breakfast, folding each napkin and container as if he could slow the morning by sheer will. "This was nice," he said at last, his voice warm with something she couldn't quite name. "I'm glad we did this."

"Me too." Ella Rose reached for the edge of the checkered cloth. They worked together, their movements easy, and in the middle their hands met and simply stayed there, neither one moving away. His thumb traced the back of her hand, a gentle stroke made rough by calluses, and when she finally looked up, his eyes were waiting for hers.

"I've got to run," Sawyer said softly, "but I can't wait to hear you sing this afternoon." He leaned down and brushed her cheek with a kiss, light as dandelion fluff on a summer breeze. "And I hope you'll save me a dance or two at the reception."

She smiled, dizzy and happy and just a little giddy. "I can do that."

He grinned. "Count on me being the guy in the back, probably with a crooked bowtie—and definitely no rhythm."

She squeezed his hand, refusing to let him go without a bit of a challenge. "Count on me noticing if you don't ask me to dance, rhythm or no rhythm."

He laughed, then let her go, his gaze lingering a moment longer before he turned and disappeared down the garden path.

Ella Rose drifted to the nearest garden bench and collapsed onto it, hands still tingling. The world shimmered. The roses were brighter, the air sweeter, the whole morning painted in watercolor pastels.

She'd spent years singing for other people's

happy endings, always just a voice in the background, a bystander. She'd never even dared let herself think about her own love story taking root.

But here, surrounded by roses and the lingering warmth of Sawyer's presence, she dared to imagine otherwise. Maybe, just maybe, this was the start of her own love story, blooming at last.

Six

ELLA ROSE

Ella Rose zipped up her dress, the deep burgundy fabric gleaming in the morning light. She caught her reflection in the mirror, her blonde waves tumbling over her shoulders, her cheeks still flushed with the happiness of that breakfast in the rose garden. The little gold karaoke trophy from last night sat on the bedside table, glinting in the sunlight, a reminder of their unexpected duet and the joy it had ignited.

Was the spark she felt actually genuine, or was it just a result of the singing, the stars, and a romantic morning brunch in a garden filled with roses? She reached for her phone. She wanted to call her sister, to get a second opinion, to anchor herself in something solid before she floated away on all these feelings.

Her finger hovered over the call button when the screen lit up with a call from her boss.

"Good morning, Dave," she said, trying not to sound as giddy as she felt.

"Rosie, where are you?" Dave's voice was sharp, nervous. "The wedding coordinator just called. She's asking when you'll arrive for the sound check."

Ella Rose glanced at the clock on the nightstand, confusion prickling at the edge of her thoughts. "I'm getting ready now. The wedding's not for another three hours."

"I know, but she wants you there now." Dave's voice rose slightly. "Look, just get over to the Bloomstead B & B as fast as you can."

Ella Rose froze, her hand gripping the phone tighter. "Bloomstead? I thought the wedding was in Bluestem. At the Whitemore Hotel."

A heavy silence stretched between them before Dave spoke again. "Rosie," he said, slow and careful, "the Jenkins-Peterson wedding is in Bloomstead, at the Bloomstead B&B. Not

Bluestem. How did you end up there? I texted you the details!"

Her heart skidded. Ella Rose scrolled through her messages with trembling hands. There it was, plain as day: Bloomstead, not Bluestem. Jenkins, not Jennings.

"I must have misread it," she said, her voice suddenly hoarse. "I saw the 'B' and just... Oh, No! Dave, I'm so sorry."

"How fast can you get there?" Dave asked, his tone all business now.

Ella Rose's hands shook as she pulled up a map on her phone. "Bloomstead is about two hours from here," she said, her chest tightening with each word. "I'm not sure I can make it in time for the ceremony."

"You need to try," Dave said, his voice insistent. "The bride specifically requested you. She heard you sing at the Norbert's wedding. She doesn't want anyone else."

"Okay. I'll be there." She wasn't sure how. The two-hour drive would be pushing it, even if she left this second.

"Great. I'll tell the coordinator you're on your way, but I won't ask them to delay the ceremony," Dave said, then ended the call.

Ella Rose sat on the edge of the bed, the phone still clutched in her hand. She stared at the text message from her boss, willing the words to rearrange themselves, to tell her she hadn't just made the worst mistake of her career. But the truth was right there in bold print: she'd gone to the wrong town.

She, who prided herself on professionalism and reliability, had botched the most basic detail of her job. Somewhere in Bloomstead, a bride was counting on her, and she was hours away.

She pressed her hands to her face, trying not to cry. "How could I have made such a careless mistake?"

And then, through the fog of remorse, she thought of Sawyer. Sawyer, who was helping his brother get ready for his wedding at this very moment. Sawyer, who had asked her to save him a dance. Sawyer, whose gentle kiss still lingered on her lips.

She didn't even have his phone number. No way to call or text him. And she was already late. She didn't have time to track him down, no time to explain.

But she couldn't leave without a word. She wouldn't.

She stood, legs trembling, and looked around the room for something—anything—that might help her get a note to Sawyer. Her eyes landed on the stack of Whitemore stationery on the writing desk by the window.

She grabbed a sheet and a pen. The first attempt ended up crumpled in her fist. Too formal. The second—too dramatic. She closed her eyes, pictured Sawyer's crooked smile over breakfast, the way he'd reached for her hand in the garden, and started over.

Dear Sawyer,

I'm so sorry to leave like this without a proper goodbye.

Ella Rose scribbled furiously, her pen pressing hard enough to indent the paper. The note was raw; an apology, an explanation, and a hope that he'd understand.

She hesitated at the end, then signed it:

Yours,

Ella Rose Tate (Rosie)

She added her phone number at the bottom, then read the note once more. It wasn't perfect, but it would have to do. The clock on the nightstand showed precious minutes had already ticked by.

Ella Rose folded the note carefully and slipped it into an envelope. She wrote Sawyer's name on the front, her normally neat handwriting slightly shaky.

Standing, she quickly surveyed the room. Her performance dress would have to do for the drive. There was no time to change. She stepped back into her driving flats and grabbed her purse, shoving her heels into it. Her overnight bag sat on the luggage rack; at least she hadn't completely settled in.

The trophy, that ridiculous, wonderful Rusty Mic, caught her eye. On impulse, she tucked it into her purse. She couldn't leave that behind.

With a deep breath that did little to steady her nerves, she picked up her purse, bag, guitar case, and the envelope, then headed for the door. At the bottom of the grand staircase, she paused, the weight of the letter heavy in her hand. She had to make sure Sawyer got it.

The lobby was empty, but she heard voices and laughter coming from a hallway behind the desk. She followed the noise, her flats quiet on the old floorboards. The scent of fresh flowers and baking pastries grew stronger as she neared the swinging door.

Inside, the kitchen was a blur of activity. Flower arrangements crowded one table, while trays of appetizers were being assembled on another. Ella Rose paused in the doorway, feeling out of place.

A woman with curly red hair was piping cream cheese onto cucumber rounds. "Can I help you?" she asked, looking up.

"I'm a guest, and I need to leave a note for someone in the wedding party before I go. I don't see LeAnne. Is she around?"

"She had to run to the store, but she'll be back soon. Who's the note for?"

"Sawyer Jennings. Do you know him?"

The woman set the piping bag down and wiped her hands. "Sure. Hang on." She leaned out the door and called, "Hey, Danny! I need you in here!"

A lanky teenager with a shock of red hair and a blue apron hurried in, dodging a floral arrangement. "What's up, Hannah?"

"This woman has something for Sawyer. Can you find him and give it to him?"

"But I'm supposed to be—"

"Don't worry. If LeAnne asks, I'll tell her you're doing a favor for me."

Ella Rose pressed the envelope into the boy's hand before he could protest further. "Thank you. I really appreciate it."

She turned and left the kitchen. The lobby was still empty. Ella Rose paused at the foot of the stairs, remembering Sawyer's gentle kiss in this very spot the night before. She allowed herself one moment to stand there, to remember, then squared her shoulders and strode out the front door.

Ella Rose walked to her car—the only Honda Civic in a lot crowded with gleaming SUVs, polished sedans, and over-sized pickup trucks—and loaded her overnight bag and guitar case into the back. She slid into the driver's seat, but her hand hovered on the key as she looked back at the Whitemore Hotel.

For a wild, reckless second, she considered staying. Calling Dave and telling him she couldn't make the Bloomstead wedding after all.

But that thought dissolved as quickly as it came. She knew she couldn't do that. Not to Dave, nor to the bride and groom who were counting on her. She couldn't let this mix-up destroy the reputation she'd spent years building.

Ella Rose backed out of the parking lot slowly, her eyes fixed on the Whitemore Hotel as if memorizing its every detail. The wraparound porch with its hanging baskets of petunias. The gleaming windows that caught the afternoon sun. The brick path that led to the rose garden where she'd found something she didn't know she'd been missing.

As she shifted into drive, movement near the side entrance caught her eye. A group of men in matching suits were standing outside, laughing and joking among themselves. Ella Rose's heart skipped. Sawyer was in the center, handsome in blue, grinning so widely she could see it from her car.

She hoped, for just a second, he might look over and see her. Their eyes would meet across the parking lot and fate would give them one last chance to say a proper goodbye.

But he didn't. His focus was on the groom, slapping him on the back and guiding him into the hotel.

"Goodbye, Sawyer," she whispered.

Ella Rose pulled out of the parking lot and onto Maple Avenue. The "Welcome to Bluestem" sign flashed past her window, and she blinked back the sting in her eyes. Then she pressed the accelerator, pointed her car toward Bloomstead, and left Bluestem—and Sawyer—behind.

Seven

SAWYER

Sawyer straightened his brother's bowtie for the third time, batting Caleb's restless hands out of the way. Around them, the ballroom was buzzing: waitstaff in crisp white shirts darted between tables, a florist hunched over a centerpiece, and relatives clustered in loud, opinionated knots. Everyone had thoughts on the seating chart, the wine, or both, and none of them were shy about sharing.

Sawyer gave the tie one last decisive tug. "Stop fidgeting. This is your big day. Try to look like you're enjoying it."

Caleb let out a shaky breath. "Easy for you to say. The ring bearer is threatening a revolt,

Amber's mom swears the flowers are a different shade of pink than we ordered, and Pastor John is nowhere to be seen. I'm supposed to enjoy this?"

Sawyer gave his brother a push. "Caleb, go. Take a walk. Hide in the bathroom. Do whatever you need to do to calm yourself down. I'll handle whatever emergency comes next."

Caleb shot him a grateful look before vanishing down the hallway toward the groom's suite. Sawyer stood still for a moment, letting the organized chaos of the ballroom swirl around him.

Rows of white chairs lined up in perfect formation, all aimed at an archway wrapped in greenery and blush-pink roses. Sunlight streamed through the tall windows, catching the vases on each table and scattering soft bursts of color across the crisp white tablecloths. Everything was perfect. A little too perfect.

Sawyer felt his shoulders knot up, an uneasy chill climbing his spine like the first gust before a summer thunderstorm. He frowned and forced himself to shake the feeling. "Get it together, Sawyer. You're as bad as Caleb."

Determined not to get swept up in worst-case scenarios, he paced the aisle, taking in the details, reminding himself this was a happy day. Nothing was going to go wrong.

His eyes landed on the small corner stage, the sound system ready and waiting. Would Rosie sing there later? The thought sent a surprising flicker of warmth through his chest.

He still couldn't believe she'd talked him into singing with her at the Rusty Spur. How in the world had she pulled that off?

"Mr. Jennings?" A voice jolted him back to the present.

He turned to see a lanky teenager in a server's uniform, face flushed, clutching a cream-colored envelope. The kid, freckles splashed across his nose, looked barely sixteen. Hannah Mitchell's little brother, Sawyer guessed, probably pressed into service to help LeAnne for the day.

"Danny, right?"

The boy nodded. "Yes, sir. Hannah asked me to give you this." He held out the envelope.

"Thanks, Danny. Tell her I appreciate it."

As Danny hurried away, Sawyer turned the

envelope over in his hands. Probably the contact information for Hannah's friend, the one who wanted an estimate for a gazebo.

"Sawyer!" He turned to see his Aunt Denise crossing the room, waving and calling to him. "The photographer wants to start the groomsmen photos in the sunroom in five minutes!"

Sawyer nodded and slipped the envelope into the inner pocket of his suit jacket. Today wasn't a day for business. Today belonged to Caleb and Amber and, if he was lucky, maybe a little to Rosie and himself.

As he headed across the ballroom toward the sunroom, Sawyer caught his reflection in a tall mirror. His blue suit fit perfectly, a minor miracle, given he'd only had one fitting. His bowtie, a shade of blue that matched the wedding colors, sat a little crooked. He straightened it, smiling as he realized how it perfectly matched the color of Rosie's eyes.

There was no sign of her yet, but it was still early. She'd mentioned needing to warm up her voice for the ceremony, so she was probably in her room, practicing. The thought of seeing her again, holding her in his arms while they danced, carried him through the sunroom door with a lighter step.

"There you are!" Caleb called, waving him over. "The rings. Do you have them? I can't remember if I gave you the rings."

Sawyer patted his side pocket, feeling the velvet box. "Right here. Safe and sound."

A wave of relief washed over Caleb's face. "I had this nightmare where I was at the altar and everyone was staring because I didn't have the rings."

"Not on my watch," Sawyer said.

Caleb nodded, some color returning to his face. "You haven't seen Amber, have you? Do you think she's ready? What if she's having second thoughts?"

Sawyer steered him toward a quiet corner, lowering his voice. "You're not supposed to see her before the ceremony, remember? And she's not having second thoughts. She's crazy about you."

Caleb hesitated. "I know. I mean, I think so. But what if she changes her mind? It happens, right? All the time, in the movies."

The photographer waved them over, impatient.

Sawyer leaned in, trying to sound reassuring. "This isn't a movie. Amber will be there, I promise. Now, smile for the camera and try not to look like you're about to face a firing squad."

Eight

SAWYER

The crowd in the ballroom continued to swell, the murmur of conversation building as more guests filed in. The scent of flowers mingled with the subtle scent of the guests' perfume. Sawyer stood near the entrance, searching every corner for a glimpse of Rosie. He wanted to wish her luck, maybe steal a quick kiss before the ceremony began.

No Rosie. But he did catch of glimpse of his brother, standing by himself, motionless except for the nervous twitch of his fingers on his cufflinks. Sawyer wove his way through the crowd to him.

"How you holding up?" Sawyer placed a steadying hand on Caleb's shoulder.

Caleb started, then laughed sheepishly. "Just running through the vows in my head." He chewed on his bottom lip. "Do you have the rings?"

Sawyer patted his side pocket. "Right here. Exactly where they were the last time you asked me. Safe and sound."

Caleb nodded, visibly relieved. "Thanks. I don't know what I'd do without you keeping track of everything."

Sawyer grinned. "That's what best men are for." He glanced around the ballroom, searching the crowd again. "By the way, where's the singer you hired?"

Caleb blinked, confusion knitting his brow. "Singer? What singer?"

"The one you hired for the ceremony. Blonde, about this tall." Sawyer held his hand at roughly Rosie's height. "Big blue eyes. Seriously great voice."

Caleb stared at Sawyer. "We didn't hire a singer, Sawyer. Live music was one of the first things we cut from the budget."

Sawyer's mind scrambled, skipping a beat. Rosie had said she was singing at Caleb's wedding. Hadn't she? Or had he just assumed that because she said she was there to sing at a wedding? Suddenly, the details felt hazy. Blurred. A whirlwind Sawyer couldn't make sense of.

Caleb frowned. "Hey. Are you all right? You look like you've seen a ghost."

Sawyer plastered a shaky smile onto his face and forced a laugh. "I'm good. But I just realized I need to check on something." He gave Caleb's shoulder a reassuring squeeze. "I'll be back before showtime."

He slipped through the crowd, scanning the faces one more time before heading to the lobby. LeAnne would know where Rosie was. She ran the hotel, managed the bookings. If anyone knew what had happened to Rosie, it would be her.

The Whitemore's lobby was a flurry of activity. Latecomers hurried toward the ballroom, guided by hotel staff in crisp black and white uniforms. The grandfather clock chimed the half hour, its sound nearly drowned out by the buzz of conversation and activity.

Sawyer made his way toward the front desk,

expecting to see LeAnne's friendly face. Instead, a man stood behind the desk.

"Rob?" Sawyer's eyebrows rose. "I didn't know you were in town."

The man looked up, his face breaking into a friendly smile. "Sawyer Jennings! Looking sharp in that suit." He reached across the polished desk to shake Sawyer's hand. "Just got in from Grand Island this morning. LeAnne roped me into desk duty so she could help with the wedding."

Sawyer clasped Rob's hand, masking his impatience with a friendly smile of his own. The Hudson siblings had grown up in Bluestem, just like he and Caleb. Rob, now an accountant in Grand Island, still co-owned the Whitemore with his sisters.

"How's life in the big city?" Sawyer asked.

"Can't complain. Business is good." Rob leaned forward and lowered his voice. "Not as exciting as your career, though. I heard you started your own business, building patios."

"It's a landscape design company," Sawyer said. "Best decision I've ever made." He glanced at his watch. Twenty minutes until the ceremony. "Listen, Rob, I'm in a bit of a hurry, and I'm looking for a woman—"

"Aren't we all?" Rob said, dryly.

Sawyer couldn't help a short laugh, despite the knot in his stomach. "No, a specific woman. Blonde hair, about this high." He held his hand at shoulder level. "Name of Rosie. She would have arrived yesterday, maybe the day before."

Rob's smile softened. "Let me check." His fingers flew across the keyboard, eyes scanning the screen. "Rosie, Rosie... Nope. I'm not seeing anyone registered under that name."

"Could she be here under a different name?" Sawyer asked. "Rose something?"

Rob continued scanning, clicking through several screens. "Sorry, Sawyer. Are you sure she was staying at the Whitemore?"

"She has to be staying here," Sawyer said. "We had breakfast together in the rose garden this morning."

Rob gave him a sympathetic shrug. "Sorry. I'm not seeing anyone named Rose or Rosie on our books for this weekend."

Sawyer ran a hand through his hair, frustration mounting. "She specifically said she was here for a wedding."

Rob tilted his head and smiled. "There's only one wedding in Bluestem this weekend, and that's your brother's. Sounds like you got your wires crossed somewhere."

The grandfather clock chimed. Fifteen minutes left.

"I need to get back," Sawyer said, his voice hollow. "If someone matching that description shows up—"

"I'll tell her you're looking for her. Now, you better get back to the ballroom. Hate to have that wedding start without you."

Sawyer nodded, forcing a smile. "You're right. Thanks for checking, Rob."

He turned from the desk, scanning the lobby one last time. The grand staircase leading to the second floor stood empty. A peek into the parlor revealed only a pair of elderly guests, quietly sipping coffee. The front doors opened and admitted a breathless couple, clearly running late, but no Rosie.

As the music swelled and guests rose to their feet, Sawyer stepped into place beside his brother. He straightened his tie, pasted on a smile, and tried to focus on the moment.

But memories of Rosie haunted him. Her laugh. The delicate brush of her fingers against his. The way she'd said she'd save a dance for him, her blue eyes shining.

As Amber made her way down the aisle and Caleb's face filled with joy, Sawyer's heart ached. Where was Rosie? And why had she left without even saying goodbye?

Nine

ELLA ROSE

Ella Rose rushed through the double doors of the Bloomstead B&B. The blast of cool air inside was a shock after the muggy July heat, but it did nothing to slow the frantic thumping of her heart. She was late, mortifyingly, unprofessionally late, and every step echoed with the reminder.

"You must be Ella!" A woman in a charcoal gray pantsuit strode toward her, clipboard in hand and wireless earpiece firmly in place. Relief washed over her face as she extended her hand. "I'm Melissa, the wedding coordinator. I am so glad to see you!"

"I am so, so sorry," Ella Rose said, shifting her guitar case to shake Melissa's hand. "There was a mix-up with the location. I thought—" She stopped herself. This wasn't the time to rehash her mistake. "No matter. I'm here now. Just tell me where you need me."

"The wedding's in the conservatory. Follow me." Melissa was already leading the way, weaving through knots of chattering guests clustered in the foyer. "We've got a mic and stand ready for you, and the sound system's live. Just plug your equipment in and you're set."

Ella Rose nodded, her hands steady even as her insides fluttered. She found the outlet, connected her amp, and set her music on the stand. "I'll do a quick sound check once I'm set up," she promised, forcing her voice to sound calm, professional.

The conservatory was gorgeous, flooded with sunlight and the scent of fresh flowers. Ivory chairs lined up in neat rows, delicate blooms at every seat, and floor-to-ceiling windows framed the bright afternoon. It was the perfect spot for a wedding: hopeful, radiant, full of promise.

But as she tuned her guitar, Ella Rose couldn't help wishing she was setting up in the ballroom of the Whitemore right now, and not here, in this beautiful conservatory in Bloomstead.

"We've got about twenty minutes until we open the room to guests," Melissa said, checking her watch. "Which means you have fifteen minutes to be completely ready."

Ella Rose nodded, propping her sheet music in place. Her fingers brushed the strings, coaxing out a tentative chord. She drew a slow breath, trying to tamp down the lingering anxiety, trying to focus on the here and now instead of the hundred miles she'd just driven, and the person she'd left behind.

She checked her phone: nothing. No calls, no texts. The silence stung more than she cared to admit.

A door opened on the other side of the conservatory. Ella Rose held her breath, foolishly hoping to see Sawyer in the doorway, flashing that irresistible grin.

But it was a woman in an elegant peach gown, her silver hair piled high, her smile polite but impersonal. The bride's mother, Ella Rose guessed; it had to be. She had performed at enough weddings to recognize both the style and the attitude.

The woman extended a manicured hand. "Ella?" Her smile was perfectly polite but stopped short of genuine warmth. "I'm Mrs. Jenkins. Miranda has been raving about you ever since she heard you sing at the Norbert wedding. She'll be relieved you made it."

Ella Rose shook the woman's hand, a fresh wave of guilt washing over her. "I'm sorry for cutting it this close. It won't affect my performance, I promise."

"I'm sure it won't," the woman said, her tone cool. "Miranda wants 'Ave Maria' for the processional, 'The Prayer' during the unity candle, and 'I Do (Cherish You)' for the recessional. Are you prepared to sing those?"

"Yes, absolutely," Ella Rose said.

The mother nodded and strode off. Alone again, Ella Rose ran through her mental checklist: music in order, amp plugged in, guitar tuned, water bottle ready. These motions were familiar, but today, each one was mechanical, as if she were simply going through the motions while the most vital part of her was still back in Bluestem.

The first guests trickled in, filling the chairs, their voices an indistinct murmur. Ella Rose played softly, gentle pre-ceremony melodies flowing from her fingers almost by rote.

The chairs gradually filled, the soft murmur of conversation swelling around her. Every time the conservatory doors opened, Ella Rose's gaze slid toward them, a stubborn, unreasonable hope flickering. But it was always another guest, another family, another reminder that she was here, and he was in Bluestem.

The wedding coordinator appeared at her side. "Bridal party's lined up. I'll give you the signal."

Ella Rose nodded, straightened her music, and inhaled slowly. When Melissa gave her the cue, she started "Ave Maria," her voice wrapping around the notes, giving them warmth and longing. The song filled the room as the bridal party glided down the aisle, sunlight turning the bride's dress of ivory lace to spun gold.

When the couple was pronounced husband and wife, Ella Rose launched into the heartfelt recessional music, the tempo matching the smiles of the newly married couple as they practically floated down the aisle, followed by their bridal party.

Ella Rose continued playing until the last

guest filed out. Only then did she allow herself a moment to breathe. Her smile faded, and she rolled her shoulders, the strain of the last three hours finally catching up to her.

"That was absolutely beautiful," an older woman said, making her way up the aisle. She paused by the mic stand, eyes bright with unshed tears.

"Thank you," Ella Rose said, the words automatic. "I'm glad you enjoyed it."

"I've never heard 'I Do' sung with such emotion. You had half the guests in tears, including me!" She patted Ella Rose's arm. "You must be in love yourself, to sing like that."

Ella Rose managed a smile, but the words hit her like a pebble in a pond, rippling through her. "I just try to do the music justice," she said, keeping her voice level, betraying nothing.

The woman smiled. "Well, you certainly did today. Thank you for helping to make my grandson's day so special."

Ella Rose gave a polite smile, but the older woman's words lingered as she packed up her things. *You must be in love yourself.* Was that what this was? This ache, this longing to see someone she'd only just met yesterday? She shook her head slightly, as if she could shake loose the thought. It wasn't possible to fall in love with someone literally overnight. Was it?

As the wedding party returned for more photographs, the wedding coordinator hurried over to her. "The reception starts in an hour at the country club," she said. "The bride is planning on you singing the first two sets during it."

"I've got the country club marked on my phone," Ella Rose said. "I'll be there."

And she would. She'd drive to the country club, set up for the reception, and be the pro she prided herself on being. She'd sing songs about passion and belonging, about finding your other half and never letting go.

And she would do her best not to think about showing up in the wrong town for the wrong wedding, or about the right guy she'd left behind.

Ten

SAWYER

Sawyer sat at the head table, watching Caleb and Amber's guests enjoy their meals with a smile he knew didn't quite reach his eyes.

White and blue decorations filled the ballroom and pink floral centerpieces graced each table. The space sparkled with twinkling fairy lights and lively conversations, but to him, it felt hollow, incomplete.

He yearned for a glimpse of one smiling face and the sound of one unforgettable laugh. He replayed their moments together again and again: the silly trophy at the Rusty Spur, breakfast among the roses that very morning. Their connection was real—he knew it was.

Then why? Why had she pretended to be a guest

at the Whitemore? Why had she said she was the singer for Caleb's wedding? And why, oh why, had she left, without saying goodbye?

"Welcome, guests!" The DJ's voice boomed over the speaker. "Please turn your attention to the head table. It's time to toast our bride and groom!"

Sawyer straightened his tie and stood up, note cards in hand. The faces of the crowd swam together as he waited for Lindsey to finish her maid of honor speech, then took the microphone from her. He cleared his throat, raised his glass, and launched into the speech he'd rehearsed a dozen times.

"When Caleb was eight years old, he told our mom he was going to marry the prettiest girl in Nebraska." The crowd chuckled right on cue. "Looks like he kept his promise, though I'm sure our mother would have appreciated it if he'd waited until after high school to start his search."

More laughter, more smiles. Sawyer delivered the lines automatically, his eyes still scanning the room. No sign of the one face he wanted to see.

"I've watched my brother grow from a kid

who couldn't tie his shoes into a man who somehow convinced this incredible woman to spend her life with him." Sawyer gestured toward Amber, who beamed up at Caleb with adoration. "And I have to say, Amber, he's a better man for having found you."

Glasses clinked. Sawyer finished his toast with words about love and partnership, though he barely remembered what he'd said. He retreated to the edge of the dance floor, content to fade into the background for a moment.

"That was a lovely speech," a voice said from behind him.

Sawyer turned.

Lindsey stood close, her bridesmaid's dress the same cornflower blue as his tie, a detail Amber had insisted upon. Her smile was pretty, but it didn't send a jolt through him the way Rosie's had.

"Thanks," he said. "Yours, too."

"The DJ says the bridal party dance is next," Lindsey said, nodding toward the dance floor. "I believe that's our cue."

He took her hand and led her onto the floor. They moved together, Lindsey chatting easily about the flowers, the ceremony, the picture-perfect weather.

Sawyer nodded and responded in all the right places, but his mind was elsewhere, replaying those last few minutes with Rosie in the garden that morning. *Had he said something wrong? Offended her in some way? It just didn't make sense.*

"Sawyer? Are you okay?" Lindsey asked.

"Sorry," he said, forcing himself to focus. "I guess I'm just tired. It's been a long day."

Lindsey's smile turned sympathetic. "I know what you mean. Amber had us up at dawn for hair and makeup. And these heels feel like medieval torture devices. I swear, my feet went numb before the two of them even said 'I do'."

Sawyer couldn't help but laugh. "At least Caleb didn't rope me into a groomsman makeover."

"Lucky you," Lindsey said. "Though I think you clean up just fine without any extra help."

He accepted the compliment with a nod, though it barely registered. He guided her through the last steps of the dance, thanked her, and stepped aside as the song ended.

He checked his watch. *Almost nine. If Rosie was coming, she would have been here by now.*

"Sawyer! Amber!" Caleb called from across the room. "Dollar dance time!"

With a nod and a wave, Sawyer and Amber made their way to the corner, where a decorative bowl sat on a small table. The DJ announced the dollar dance to the crowd, and guests began to line up for a turn on the dance floor with Caleb or Amber. As best man, Sawyer collected for Caleb, while Lindsey managed Amber's line.

Most people moved through the line quickly, dropping bills and trading jokes. When Aunt Martha's turn came, she fixed Sawyer with a perceptive look.

"You're looking lost, dear. Wedding making you sentimental?"

"Just tired," Sawyer said, the excuse wearing thin even to him. "Been a long day."

Aunt Martha clucked her tongue. "Well, perk up. We'll be dancing at your wedding soon, I'm sure." She dropped her money in the bowl and moved to where Caleb danced with her sister, Aunt Bess.

Sawyer barked a humorless laugh. *His wedding? Not if he kept scaring off women before things even got started.* He continued collecting dollars, each bill a small, crisp reminder of the dance he wouldn't be sharing with Rosie tonight.

After ten minutes, Sawyer handed the job to another groomsman. He needed air, space, and a moment to pull himself together. This whole situation was absurd. He'd known Rosie less than two days. There was no logical reason for her absence to sting so much.

But it did.

He walked toward the ballroom exit and stepped onto the wraparound porch. The evening air was cool against his face, carrying the sweet scent of the roses that had surrounded them that morning. Above, stars dotted the clear Nebraska sky, the same stars they'd admired on their walk home from the Rusty Spur.

"There you are," Lindsey said, joining him at the rails of the porch. "Caleb's looking for you. They're about to cut the cake."

"Sorry." Sawyer rubbed a hand across his jaw. "Just needed a breather."

Lindsey studied him, head tilted. "You know, Amber said you might be a tough nut to crack, but I didn't expect you to disappear mid-reception."

Sawyer raised an eyebrow. "A tough nut? Is that what she said?"

Lindsey nodded, her smile playful. "I think her exact words were 'stubborn and impossible.'"

Sawyer laughed, and for the first time that night, it was real. "That sounds more like Amber."

Lindsey stepped closer, her expression serious. "Look. I know Amber was a bit heavy-handed with the setup. But you seem like a nice guy, and I'd be lying if I said I wasn't interested."

Sawyer hesitated, torn between politeness and honesty. "Lindsey—"

Lindsey smiled, taking a step back. "I also know when not to push. If you decide you'd like to see me sometime, Amber has my number." She paused, hand on the doorknob. "Now, let's go eat some cake!"

Sawyer followed her back inside with a curious blend of guilt and relief. The rest of the reception passed in a blur: laughter, cake, the bouquet toss, the garter toss. Sawyer went through the motions, his smile fixed, his eyes no longer searching the crowd.

By eleven, most of the older guests were gone, leaving the younger crowd to enjoy the DJ's increasingly upbeat selections. Sawyer nursed his second whiskey in a quiet corner, watching couples sway under the dimmed lights.

Caleb and Amber remained at the center of the dance floor, her head resting on his shoulder as they moved in slow circles. Around them, a few determined dancers persisted: Lindsey dancing with a groomsman, his parents swaying to their own rhythm, a cluster of Amber's college friends giggling as they moved together in an uncoordinated group.

Sawyer swirled the amber liquid in his glass, watching the light play through it. His eyes burned; exhaustion tugged at his limbs.

"Not much of a dancer, eh?" Uncle Joe, his father's older brother, stood beside him, ruddy-faced and cheerful despite the late hour.

"I'm just taking a break," Sawyer said, forcing a smile.

"Breaks are for old folks like me." Uncle Joe clapped Sawyer on the back with enough force to make him take half a step forward. "So what's eating you. And don't say 'nothing.' You've been moping around all night."

Sawyer hesitated, unsure how to explain something he barely understood himself. How could he tell his uncle he was upset about the disappearance of a woman he'd known for less than two days? A woman who, according to the hotel records, didn't even exist?

"There was this girl," he said at last, every word reluctant. "I thought she was going to be here, but she didn't show. Doesn't matter now."

"You were ghosted, huh?" Uncle Joe sipped his drink. "Happens to the best of us. Of course, we just called it being stood up."

Ghosted? Is that what this is? The word hit hard, sharp and sudden. Heat rose under Sawyer's collar as anger threatened to chase away the sadness.

"Yeah, well, lesson learned," Sawyer muttered, draining the last of his whiskey.

Uncle Joe studied him for a long moment. "Don't let one disappointment harden you, son. That's a bitter road to walk."

"I'm fine," Sawyer said, even as his mind began spinning a new narrative, one where Rosie had been playing some kind of sick game with him.

He'd opened up to her about leaving his finance career, about finding joy in creating outdoor spaces. He'd told her things he rarely shared with anyone, and she'd listened with those attentive eyes that made him feel like everything he said mattered.

But if she'd really cared, wouldn't she have said goodbye? Left a message? Something?

"Your aunt's waving me over. Looks like she's ready to leave," Uncle Joe said. "But you? You should try to enjoy what's left of the night, Sawyer. Your brother only gets married once. At least, that's the plan..." He walked away, laughing at his own joke.

Sawyer nodded, barely registering his uncle's words. His mind was too busy dissecting every moment with Rosie, but this time through a cynical lens.

Her surprise when he'd mentioned Caleb's wedding. *Had that been real, or just good acting?* The way she'd coerced him onto the stage to sing a duet with her. *Was that manipulation, rather than spontaneity?* Even their breakfast in the rose garden seemed suspect now. *Had she been laughing at him the whole time, planning her mysterious exit while he sat there, completely captivated?*

"Country bumpkin," he whispered under his breath, the words sour. *Was that all he'd been to her? A little local color? An amusing way to pass the time?*

"All right, folks, we're coming to the end of the evening. Let's get everyone on the floor for one last dance before we say goodbye to the happy couple!"

Following the D.J.'s announcement, a slow, familiar melody rose from the speakers. Sawyer froze. He hadn't noticed this song in the lineup earlier, but there was no mistaking the opening notes of "Keeper of the Stars." Everything around him faded as Tracy Byrd's gravelly tone filled the room.

Sawyer closed his eyes, letting the music wash over him. *Why this song? The one song that seemed tailor-made for his night with Rosie?*

Lindsey appeared at his side and reached for his arm. Sawyer let her pull him toward the dance floor.

"I love this song," Lindsey said as they

swayed together. "Thank you for dancing with me."

Sawyer glanced down at Lindsey, her open expression tugging at his conscience. He searched for words that wouldn't mislead her about his intentions, but also wouldn't make him sound like a complete jerk. He would never want to hurt someone the way Rosie had hurt him, even unintentionally.

He finally settled for, "It is a great song. Thanks for asking me."

The song ended, and the lights came up. LeAnne appeared with two boxes of bubble wands that glowed with tiny LED lights. "Sawyer! Lindsey! It's time for the big send-off! Can you help us pass these out?"

Sawyer and Lindsey each took a box, joining the other members of the bridal party in handing bubble wands to the remaining guests. The warm glow from mason jar lanterns illuminated the path outside as Amber and Caleb made their way through a tunnel of bubbles and cheers.

A distant clock chimed midnight. Sawyer closed his eyes for a moment, allowing himself one last indulgence: the memory of Rosie standing on stage at the Rusty Spur, her voice filling the room, her eyes finding his in the crowd.

It had almost been a fairy tale moment. But he wasn't a prince. And this wasn't a story with glass slippers and happily-ever-afters. Whatever magic they'd shared, it was obvious that for her, it was over. And he wasn't the kind of guy to chase after someone who didn't want to be found.

So starting tomorrow, he'd do what he did best. He'd get up and go to work. And he'd forget all about Rosie and her blonde hair and her blue eyes and their one perfect night under the stars.

Eleven

ELLA ROSE

The banquet hall of the Bloomstead Country Club glittered, strung with a thousand tiny bulbs overhead. The faux-Victorian opulence—gold-threaded drapes, pristine tablecloths, and crystal vases full of flowers—gave the reception an air of sophistication that Ella Rose found both impressive and, if she were honest, a little nauseating.

She checked her phone. Six hours since she'd left Bluestem. Six hours since she'd written that note for Sawyer. Six hours, and still nothing. No text, no missed call, nothing to show he'd even noticed she was gone.

"Ladies and gentlemen," the DJ called out from his booth, his voice full of energy, "please welcome Mr. and Mrs. Cameron Peterson!" The crowd erupted in applause as the newlyweds swept into the hall, beaming beneath the lights.

Ella Rose took her place on the little stage they'd set up for her. "This first song is dedicated to the happy couple," she said, her professional voice firmly in place. The opening notes of "Could I Have This Dance" floated across the room, and Ella Rose let the music fill the emptiness she felt inside.

Miranda and Cameron glided along the polished wooden floor, their movements graceful despite Cameron's obvious nervousness. Ella Rose watched them as she sang, noting the way Miranda looked up at her new husband with trust and adoration.

As the song continued, the dance floor filled: first the parents, then the entire wedding party. Ella Rose's gaze wandered over the dancers, pausing for a moment on the maid of honor and the best man. They danced with the slight awkwardness of people just getting to know each other. The man said something that made the woman throw her head back and laugh, unguarded and real.

The sight triggered a memory of Sawyer at

the Rusty Spur, how his eyes had crinkled at the corners when she'd teased him about his singing. The memory was so vivid it almost hurt.

She finished the song to gentle applause. "Thank you. Let's pick up the tempo a bit, shall we?"

For the next hour, she sang everything from love ballads to energetic dance hits. Couples old and young filled the floor. Bridesmaids kicked off their shoes, groomsmen loosened their ties, and the room buzzed with laughter and music. Ella Rose provided the soundtrack to their celebration, all while trying not to imagine another wedding reception two hours away.

When her first set ended, she slipped away from the mic and over to the small table reserved for her in the corner. She sat, letting her shoulders relax for the first time all night. A server appeared almost instantly, balancing a plate stacked with roast beef, garlic mashed potatoes, and colorful vegetables.

Ella Rose thanked him, a pang of hunger reminding her she hadn't eaten since breakfast. That sunlit meal with Sawyer in the rose garden felt a lifetime ago.

The memory brought a sharp ache. She

picked at her food, her appetite gone. Across the room, she could see Miranda and Cameron, radiant and glowing, walking around between the tables.

Ella Rose glanced at her phone again. Still blank. With a small sigh, she set it down and took a few obligatory bites. Her next set would require energy.

"You have an amazing voice."

Ella Rose looked up. A groomsman stood by her table, holding two glasses of champagne. He had sandy hair and a wide, open smile.

She blinked. "Thank you."

He offered her a glass. "Seriously. When you sang 'Make You Feel My Love,' I got chills."

Ella Rose accepted the champagne, careful to keep her smile polite. "That's very kind of you to say." She took a small sip, letting the bubbles tickle her nose before setting it back down. She never drank during performances.

"I'm Jason. College roommate of the groom." He set his own glass on the table next to hers and nodded toward the dance floor, where couples swayed to the DJ's music beneath the twinkling lights. "I know you're working, but would you dance with me? Just one song?"

The request was so earnest, so polite, Ella Rose almost said yes. But her mind flashed to Sawyer: his smile as he watched her sing, their voices intertwining as they sang together, her hand in his as they strolled from the Rusty Spur to the Whitemore.

"I should probably stay with my equipment," she said. "But thank you for asking."

The groomsman shrugged good-naturedly. "I understand. Maybe later, then? The reception goes until midnight."

Ella Rose shook her head. "I need to pack up right after my next set. It's a long drive home."

"Where's home?"

"Lincoln."

"I actually live in Omaha," Jason said, a hopeful note in his voice. "Maybe I could get your number?"

Ella Rose hesitated. A month ago, she might have been interested. But now, with the memory of Sawyer's kiss still fresh, the idea of giving this handsome man her number just felt wrong. "I'm sorry. I'm... seeing someone," she said, the words coming out before she could rethink them.

"Lucky guy," Jason said, a little wistful. "Well, if things don't work out..." He pulled a business card from his pocket and set it on her table.

She watched him go, wondering why she wasn't more interested. He was handsome, polite, everything she should want.

But his smile was just a smile. His eyes were just eyes. They didn't pull her in or make her breath catch like Sawyer's did. Last night at the Whitemore, Sawyer had barely introduced himself before they were talking as if they'd known each other for years.

There was an ease, a spark, something between the two of them she couldn't quite name but couldn't forget. With Jason, she felt only the weight of obligation, like his attention should flatter her, but it didn't. Like she should want to tuck his card in her purse, but she didn't.

A hush fell across the hall. The newlyweds stood before a three-tiered cake, the surface frosted smooth and topped with the same peach roses that filled the vases on every table. Miranda and Cameron joined hands around the silver cake knife, their faces close as they made the first cut.

Ella Rose watched them feed each other small bites; Miranda with a delicate smile,

Cameron with a touch more frosting than intended, making his bride laugh and the guests cheer. It was a sweet, familiar ritual, yet tonight it made her chest ache with a strange, hollow feeling.

The bouquet toss was next. Ella Rose took advantage of the flurry of activity to check her phone one more time. Still nothing. She tucked it back into her small purse with a sigh.

When her break ended, she returned to the stage and chose slower, more romantic songs. The lights dimmed, and couples filled the dance floor, some snuggling close, others just holding hands and swaying gently to the music. Miranda and Cameron whispered to each other, the bride's head on her husband's shoulder. Older couples moved with a simple grace, years of shared dances clear in their steps.

"This next song is for anyone who's ever fallen in love unexpectedly," Ella Rose said into the microphone, surprised to find her voice trembling a little at the words. As she played the opening chords of "Can't Help Falling in Love," she felt her voice deepen, coloring each line with the longing she'd tried so hard to hide all night.

Champagne flutes clinked at tables. Couples

held each other close. Friends sang along, arms around each other, voices blending with hers. Ella Rose watched it all, her voice carrying the melody while her mind replayed Sawyer's request to save him a dance or two at the reception.

Who was he dancing with now?

For her last song, the couple had chosen "What a Wonderful World." Ella Rose poured everything she had into it, her voice filling the hall and reaching every corner. An elderly man dabbed away tears from his wife's cheek. The bride rested her head on her new husband's shoulder, eyes closed in contentment.

As the last note faded, applause rippled through the room. Ella Rose's voice felt dry and raw, like sun-baked earth after a summer drought. She closed her eyes and let the warmth of the audience's clapping linger for a moment before lowering the mic and exhaling slowly.

She thanked the guests, congratulated the couple once more, and announced that the DJ would take over for the rest of the evening. As the guests turned their attention elsewhere, Ella Rose let her professional smile fade.

It was nearly ten when Ella Rose finally

loaded the last of her equipment into her Honda Civic. The reception was still going strong inside, but her role was complete. She slid into the driver's seat, the map glowing on her phone, the cursor blinking.

She hesitated, then typed "Bluestem, Nebraska" into the search bar. The route popped up: 113 miles. If she left now, she could be there before midnight. She could see Sawyer, explain everything face to face.

The idea made her heart race with equal parts excitement and anxiety. Would he smile when he saw her again? Or would he be angry that she'd left this morning without a proper goodbye? Why, oh why, hadn't he called?

The questions spun through her like leaves swirling in an autumn breeze, impossible to catch, impossible to stop. Her heart ached with the longing to hear his voice, to know their magical night had meant as much to him as it did to her.

Ella Rose took a steadying breath. Tonight was his brother's wedding. He was at the Whitemore, busy doing best man things: smiling for pictures, clinking glasses, maybe even offering a toast. The sensible thing—the only thing—was to drive back to her apartment in Lincoln, crawl into her own bed, and wait. If Sawyer wanted to contact her, he would.

Ella Rose stared at the stars twinkling brilliantly above her. These were the same stars she and Sawyer had admired during their walk back from the Rusty Spur. A single bright star caught her eye. She hadn't made a wish on a star in years, but tonight she couldn't help herself.

"Please let Sawyer call me," she whispered, the words barely more than a breath. "Please." It felt silly, foolish even, but speaking the words out loud somehow made the wish more possible.

Her phone buzzed. Ella Rose nearly dropped it in her rush to check the screen, but it wasn't Sawyer. It was Dave, her boss.

"Rosie, just talked to the wedding planner. She was over the moon about your performance. Said she's going to recommend you to all her brides."

Ella Rose felt her mouth curl into a tired smile. "That's wonderful, Dave. Thanks for letting me know."

"See you next week," he said, and ended the call.

Ella Rose leaned her head against the

steering wheel, letting the disappointment settle over her. The dashboard clock glowed 10:18 PM. A wave of exhaustion washed over her. The rush to Bloomstead, the performance, the emotional weight of waiting for a call that never came.

She reached into her purse, pulled out the Rusty Mic, and set it gently on the passenger seat. She plugged in her phone, set the navigation for Lincoln, and started the engine. Ninety minutes. She'd be home before midnight.

As she merged onto the highway, Ella Rose kept her eyes on the road. But her heart was two hours away, singing a karaoke duet with a man she feared she might never see again.

Twelve

ELLA ROSE

Ella Rose balanced her guitar case on one shoulder and nudged open her apartment door with her hip. Her overnight case bumped along behind her, catching on the rug just inside the entryway. She flicked on the light with her elbow. The old overhead fixture flickered, then filled the little space with a soft, steady glow. She set her guitar case just inside the apartment door and exhaled a shaky breath.

She knew she should eat something, but the thought of food made her stomach wretch. Instead, she rolled her overnight case into the bedroom. She checked her phone one more time. No missed calls. No new messages. Not even a spam text.

She stared at the blank screen for a moment before tossing it onto the comforter with a sigh. She grabbed her pajamas and headed for the shower, cranking the water as hot as she could stand. For a few minutes, she just stood there, letting the steam rise around her, washing away the last traces of hairspray, makeup, and perfume. If only the water could rinse away the ache in her chest, too.

Back in her room, she started unpacking. It was something to do with her hands, even if her mind was miles away. She hung up the clothes she hadn't worn, tossed the rest into the hamper, and lined up her toiletries on the bathroom shelf.

The last thing Ella Rose unpacked was the Rusty Mic trophy. She turned it over in her hands, felt the weight of it, let her fingers trace the cheap gold-painted plastic. Then she set it on her dresser, right in the center where the morning sun would hit it.

Visible from both her bed and her living room, it would be a tangible reminder that her time with Sawyer hadn't been a dream. That their connection had been real, despite the fact her phone remained stubbornly silent.

Ella Rose crawled under the covers, pulling the comforter up to her chin despite the mild summer night. Sleep came in fits and starts, anxious dreams of missed performances and angry brides, mixed with images of Sawyer, always just out of reach, lost in a crowd.

Morning arrived with harsh sunlight and the persistent chirp of birds outside her window. Ella Rose rolled over, her hand automatically reaching for her phone. Still nothing. She let the phone fall with a dull thud onto the nightstand and forced herself out of bed.

The coffeemaker gurgled, filling the apartment with the smell of fresh coffee. Ella Rose leaned on the kitchen counter, staring out the window at the street below: a neighbor walking his dog, a delivery truck idling at the curb, a couple arguing over who would drive.

The world kept spinning, but Ella Rose felt trapped, caught between the weekend's memories and today's doubts.

The coffee finished brewing, filling her apartment with its rich aroma. She filled her mug and wandered to the living room, settling onto the piano bench. The keys felt cool and familiar beneath her fingers, and she played a string of almost-blues, lingering on the pauses between chords, letting their weight fill up the room and echo a little longer than usual.

From this angle, she could see the Rusty Mic on her dresser. The morning sun caught it just as she'd imagined, turning the cheap gold paint a warm, blinding yellow.

She sipped her coffee, her mind turning over the idea of calling the Whitemore Hotel. It would be easy enough. "Hello, this is Ella Tate. I'm trying to reach Sawyer Jennings. Do you have his number?" Simple words that stuck in her throat like peanut butter.

Ella Rose looked out the window where the sky was changing from pink to blue. She wouldn't be that girl. The one who chased after a guy because he didn't contact her on her timeline. She'd left her number in the note. The ball was in his court now.

Maybe it was better this way. Less complicated. They lived hours apart. They'd spent less than twenty four hours together. Real relationships took work, compromise, sacrifice. Maybe the universe had saved them both from the disappointment of reality.

Her eyes strayed to the trophy once more,

then she turned back to the piano. Time to focus on the one thing that never let her down: her music. She would work on some new songs, book a few extra gigs. That would keep her mind off Sawyer, at least for a little while.

The days blurred together. Weeks went by with still no word from Sawyer. The city shifted from summer to fall, and somewhere between the first Husker game and the last official day of summer, Ella Rose let her friend Katie set her up on a blind date.

"He teaches music at one of the local high schools," Katie said, sipping her latte. "Plays piano, guitar, and I think trumpet. Super sweet guy. Cute, too!" She stirred her drink, her voice rising with excitement. "You'll like him. I promise!"

Ella Rose raised an eyebrow, but Katie's expression was unyielding. *Why not? Maybe Katie was right. Maybe she would like him.* Ella Rose gave in. "All right. One dinner."

Katie nearly crowed. "Friday at seven? I'll text him your number."

Kyle called the next night, and they made plans to meet at Vincenzo's, the Italian place downtown, at six. Ella Rose wasn't sure if she was happy or just trying to be. She picked out a blue dress for the date and tried to keep her expectations low.

He was waiting outside when Ella Rose arrived. Katie hadn't exaggerated. He was good-looking, with neat dark hair, warm brown eyes, and dimples when he smiled.

"Rosie?" he asked. His handshake was warm, his cologne subtle. All good signs, Ella Rose thought.

"Katie says you teach music?" Ella Rose asked, as they settled into their chairs.

Kyle nodded, his eyes lighting up. "Eleven years now. Started at middle school, moved to high school about five years ago." He leaned forward slightly. "Nothing beats seeing a student finally get it after weeks of struggling."

Ella Rose smiled at the passion in his voice. "Music is so important for kids," she said.

"It is. But I have to admit I'm a little jealous of what you do. Performing. Being on stage. I miss that."

The conversation flowed easily through dinner. Kyle had funny stories about teaching, thoughtful questions about her gigs, and a genuine love for classic country. But by dessert, Ella Rose realized she was finishing his sentences in her head. Kyle was nice, but it felt more like talking to a friend than starting a new romance.

After dinner, Kyle walked her to her car. "I had a great time tonight," he said, when they stopped beside her Honda. "I'd like to see you again, if you're interested."

Ella Rose looked at him. Handsome. Kind. Stable. Shared interests. No red flags. "That would be nice," she heard herself say, kindness winning out over the honest truth: *I'm sorry, but you're not him.*

Kyle smiled, clearly pleased. "Great. I'll call you."

He leaned in for a goodnight kiss; brief, pleasant, skillful even. Ella Rose returned it automatically, waiting for a flutter, a spark, anything to show that her heart was engaged. Nothing. Just emptiness and a little guilt for not feeling more.

"Drive safe," he said, stepping back.

"You, too," she said, slipping into her car with a manufactured smile.

They went out two more times. Coffee and a quick walk through a music store, then a concert at the Lied Center. Each date was comfortable, friendly, fun. But comfort wasn't the same as chemistry, and Ella Rose knew it. After the Lied Center concert, she told Kyle she wasn't ready for a new relationship. He nodded, almost relieved, as if he'd sensed it all along.

It was almost midnight when she got home that night. She kicked off her heels just inside the door. The moonlight slipped through the blinds, striping the carpet and walls with silver.

She should be tired. It had been a busy week. Three performances earlier in the week, followed by tonight's date with Kyle, but her mind buzzed with restless energy. Sleep would be elusive tonight; she could feel it.

Ella Rose set her purse on the coffee table, grabbed a glass of water, and wandered to the piano.

She didn't bother with the lights. The moon lit the keys in a soft, silvery glow, and she imagined she was playing outside under an open night sky.

The melody that emerged wasn't one she recognized. Not a song she sang for a wedding or a gig at a coffee shop, nor anything she'd written before. It came from somewhere deep, somewhere raw and honest that she'd been avoiding for weeks. The notes were sweet but tinged with melancholy, like remembering something beautiful that couldn't be recaptured.

Ella Rose closed her eyes, letting the music guide her. Words floated through her mind. Bits and pieces at first, then whole lines that matched the rise and fall of the melody.

A brief embrace of pure delight.

A memory etched in a starlit night.

She scribbled lyrics into her notebook, adjusting the phrasing, matching words to notes until they fit together like puzzle pieces.

I'm warmed by thoughts of what we shared.

And wonder if you know or care.

Tears streamed down her cheeks, silent and hot. She didn't try to stop them. Didn't even want to. Instead, she channeled the emotion back into the song, her voice stronger with each line.

She changed a word here, added a note there.

She lost track of time. Hours passed. The process was cathartic, transforming her pain into art.

By the time she settled on the final words of the chorus, the sky outside was pale with the rising of the sun.

Some fires burn a single time,
And then they're gone, but leave behind
A single spark, a quiet flame —
And nothing ever feels the same.

Ella Rose slumped on the piano bench, exhausted. The song was good, possibly the best she'd ever written. It captured everything: the magic of finding Sawyer, the ache of losing him, the truth that some things aren't meant to be.

She closed her notebook, set it on top of the piano, stood, and stretched. She'd spent too long looking backward, checking her phone, scanning crowds for a face she might never see again. It was time to move on.

With new resolve, Ella Rose walked to the dresser where the Rusty Mic still caught the morning light. She picked it up, cuddled it to her chest, and smiled a bittersweet, gentle smile.

Then she opened the bottom drawer and made a little space among her old scarves and winter gloves. Not thrown away, but not on display either. A memento of something sweet but finished. The drawer slid shut with a gentle click.

Ella Rose returned to the living room. She closed her notebook and set it on the top of her piano, where it would wait for her while she grabbed a few hours of much-needed sleep. She had a busy day ahead. An afternoon meeting with Dave, a department store performance, and a wedding consultation with a bride.

And although a part of her would always ache for the possibility of what might have been, she would let that longing live in her music and not in the hope of a call that would never come.

Thirteen

SAWYER

The bell above the door chimed softly as Sawyer stepped into the shop, the familiar scent of starch and pressed cotton instantly filling his nose. Fluorescent lights hummed overhead, making the linoleum floor shine. A row of winter coats hung neatly on the rack, a silent reminder that Christmas was coming fast.

He should have picked up his suit months ago. Right after Caleb's wedding, in fact. But every time he thought about making the trip to Grand Island to the cleaners, he'd find an excuse to skip the errand.

He knew why. The moment he saw that blue suit again, all those memories of Rosie would come flooding back. Her laughter. Her singing. Her hand in his as they strolled back to the Whitemore. The slow, dawning realization that their story was over before it had truly begun, and the bitter aftertaste of questions left unanswered.

Sawyer had tried everything to forget her. He'd thrown himself into landscaping projects, working double shifts until he fell into bed, too tired to think. Four months should have been enough time to move on.

But no matter how hard he tried, nothing erased the memory of her smile, or the way her hand had felt in his. Her disappearance had become a dull ache, an invisible splinter he'd learned to work around but never managed to extract.

Now, thanks to Amber's not-so-subtle reminder about LeAnne's Christmas open house and her "no denim" dress code, he couldn't avoid the cleaners, or that blue suit, any longer.

The woman behind the counter was older, her silver hair pulled back in a neat bun. "Name?" she asked, already reaching for the ticket rack.

"Jennings. Sawyer Jennings."

She shuffled through a row of paper tickets, mumbling the names under her breath. "Jennings, Jennings... Oh! Here we are. Just a minute, Hon."

She disappeared into the forest of plastic-wrapped garments. Sawyer distracted himself by mentally reviewing the holiday decorations for the town square. The mayor had specifically requested something "festive but tasteful" for the holiday lighting ceremony next week. Sawyer was mentally calculating how many strands of lights they'd need for the gazebo when the clerk returned with his suit and shirt in a plastic bag, along with a white envelope.

"Found this in the pocket during cleaning," she said, handing the envelope to him.

"Thanks," Sawyer said. He frowned at his name, written clearly on the front in looping handwriting that didn't look familiar. For a moment, something tugged at the back of his mind, vague and fleeting, a fuzzy memory of someone handing him an envelope at Caleb's wedding. Something to do with a request from a new client. But the thought dissolved before he could fully grab it.

He paid for the cleaning and headed out to his truck. Gray clouds hung low overhead, promising snow before the day was out. Sawyer started the engine, then glanced at the envelope on the passenger seat. Just a simple white envelope, his name on the front.

With a shrug, he slid his finger under the flap and tore it open. Inside was a folded piece of paper—hotel stationery from the Whitemore.

Dear Sawyer,

I'm so sorry to leave like this without saying a proper goodbye.

Sawyer's heart slammed against his ribcage. He read the first lines again, not quite believing what he was seeing. It was from her. From Rosie. After four months of silence, of wondering, of gradually convincing himself it had all been some sort of game, here was her explanation in black and white.

His eyes raced across the page, devouring her words.

There's been a terrible mix-up with my work. It turns out the wedding I was hired to sing for is actually in Bloomstead, not Bluestem. I only discovered this now, and I have to leave immediately if I want to have any hope of making it to that wedding on time.

I want you to know that these past two days together have meant more to me than I can express in this rushed note. From karaoke at the Rusty Spur to breakfast in the rose garden, every moment with you has been unexpected and wonderful. Thank you for showing me the stars over Bluestem.

Yours,

Ella Rose Tate (Rosie)

Below her name was a Lincoln phone number.

Sawyer stared at the paper, his hands trembling. Ella Rose Tate. Her real name was Ella Rose. And she hadn't ghosted him or played him for a fool. She'd been in the wrong town for the wrong wedding, and when she discovered her mistake, she'd left a note explaining everything.

A note that had sat in his suit pocket for four months while he built a wall of resentment and disappointment around himself.

"No! No, no, no," he whispered, letting his head fall back against the headrest. The realization hit him like a physical blow. All this time, she'd probably been waiting for him to call.

Four months of pushing away thoughts of her, of throwing himself into work, of telling himself it was better this way. Four months that could have been something completely different.

Sawyer read the letter again, slowly this time. There was genuine regret in her hurried explanation, real feeling in her description of their time together. And her signature—"Yours"—held a promise. A promise he hadn't dared hope for since that morning in the rose garden.

Outside, the first snowflakes of the season were falling, tiny white specks against his windshield. Sawyer didn't notice. He was too busy rereading the note, committing her phone number to memory. Ella Rose Tate from Lincoln. The woman whose laugh had haunted his dreams. The woman who sang like an angel and saw something in him worth sharing her dreams with.

The woman who had never meant to disappear from his life at all.

A mixture of emotions coursed through him. Relief that she hadn't rejected him. Frustration at the cosmic joke of the letter sitting unread in his pocket for months. Regret for the time they'd lost. And beneath it all, a sharp, reckless thrill of hope.

Sawyer's phone sat in the cupholder, suddenly the most important object in his world. He picked it up, fingers hovering over the keypad. What would he say after all this time? Would she even want to hear from him? Had she moved on, assumed his silence meant disinterest?

Only one way to find out. Sawyer took a deep breath and began pushing buttons, then listened as the phone began to ring.

Once. Twice. Three times.

Then a click and a recorded message. "You've reached Ella Tate! I can't come to the phone right now, but please leave a message and I'll get back to you as soon as I can."

The sound of her voice, even in recorded form, made his chest tighten. He closed his eyes, letting the warmth of it fill him, a balm for the months of confusion and hurt. But it was over too soon, the beep sounding before he'd even gathered his thoughts.

Sawyer hung up without leaving a message. He couldn't leave a voicemail. He needed to see her, to look into her eyes and know that what they'd shared was real.

He tapped the steering wheel, a plan already

forming. This wasn't over. Not by a long shot. He had her name, her number, and the truth.

He shifted the truck into gear. Sometimes life gave you a second chance, and he wasn't about to waste his.

Fourteen

ELLA ROSE

Ella Rose draped the last strand of silver tinsel across her small Christmas tree, stepping back to assess her handiwork.

December had arrived with its particular blend of nostalgia and anticipation, dusting Lincoln with the first snow of the season. She'd spent the morning transforming her apartment into a modest winter wonderland: candles on the windowsills, a wreath on the door, and this slightly crooked tree that filled the room with the scent of pine while shedding its needles at an alarming rate. The radio played "White Christmas" softly in the background, Bing Crosby's smooth voice a familiar comfort.

It had been more than four months since

Bluestem. Four months since Sawyer. Her calendar had become a patchwork of performances, and she accepted every invitation that promised a stage and a paycheck. She'd crooned "At Last" for tearful newlyweds, provided background melodies for corporate cocktail chatter, and serenaded wine-tasters as the sun set over vineyard rows.

The only silver lining was that "A Single Spark" had become something of a signature piece. Audiences connected with it in a way they never had with her other original compositions. There was something about raw honesty wrapped in a melody that resonated with people. Even Dave noticed the difference.

"Whatever inspired that song," he'd said, "hold onto it. That's the real deal."

If only he knew.

Ella Rose turned away from the tree and walked to the kitchen to brew herself a cup of peppermint tea. She checked the calendar on her refrigerator, reviewing her upcoming bookings. A holiday party at the Eagles Club on Friday night, then the rest of her weekend was blissfully empty. A chance to catch up on laundry and maybe work on a new arrangement for an upcoming New Year's Eve performance.

The phone rang, startling her. Ella Rose reached for it, expecting her mother's voice. She was overdue for their weekly call.

"Hello?"

"Ella Tate?" The voice was warm, feminine, and vaguely familiar.

"Yes, this is she."

"This is LeAnne Hudson, from the Whitemore Hotel in Bluestem. I hope I'm not catching you at a bad time."

The Whitemore. Just hearing the name sent a cascade of memories through Ella Rose's mind. The elegant staircase. The cozy parlor. The Jeri Southern room. And Sawyer. She tightened her grip on the mug, its warmth anchoring her to the present.

"LeAnne, hello. This is a surprise." She kept her voice light, professional. "How are you?"

"I'm wonderful, thank you. I'm calling because we're in a bit of a bind here. Our annual Christmas Open House is this Saturday evening, and our regular performer canceled because of a family emergency." LeAnne's voice was warm but hurried. "I wondered if there is any possibility that you might be available."

Ella Rose sank onto a kitchen chair. This weekend. She looked at her calendar again, at the blissfully empty weekend that now felt like a trap.

"This Saturday? That's …that's very short notice." Ella Rose rubbed her thumb against the ceramic mug. Go back to Bluestem? Her stomach tightened at the thought.

"I know, and I'm terribly sorry about that. We'd pay you well, of course, and provide the room. The Jeri Southern is actually available again, if you liked it last time."

Ella Rose closed her eyes. The Jeri Southern room, with its view of the garden. "I'm curious. How did you think to call me?"

There was a brief pause before LeAnne answered. "One of our regular patrons mentioned having heard you sing somewhere and thought you'd be perfect. They were quite insistent that I try to reach you."

A regular patron. Ella Rose's pulse quickened. Outside, snow drifted lazily past the glass.

Could it be Sawyer? No. If he'd wanted to

contact her, he would have months ago. She'd left her number in her note. He hadn't called.

"What would the performance entail?" she asked, surprising herself.

"Just two hours of Christmas music in our ballroom, from seven to nine on Saturday evening. The guests will be mingling, enjoying refreshments. It's very casual, though people do dress up a bit."

Ella Rose pressed her forehead against the cool windowpane. Two competing desires battled within her. Part of her wanted to decline, to protect herself from the inevitable pain a return to Bluestem would bring.

But another part, the part that had written "A Single Spark" in the wee hours of the morning, yearned for one last look at the town where she'd left a piece of her heart.

"Ella? Are you still there?" LeAnne's voice pulled her back to the present.

"Yes, sorry," Ella Rose said, clearing her throat. "I was just checking my calendar." She took a deep breath. "And yes, I'd be happy to perform at your Open House." The words tumbled out before she could second-guess them.

"Oh, that's wonderful news!" The relief in LeAnne's voice was unmistakable, and a little infectious.

They spent the next few minutes discussing the details: technical requirements, song expectations, payment. Ella Rose jotted notes on a notepad, her handwriting more uneven than usual.

"Is there anything else you'd like to know?" LeAnne asked.

Ella Rose hesitated. She wanted to ask about Sawyer. But she swallowed the words. "No, I think we've covered everything. I'll see you Saturday afternoon."

"Perfect. I'll have the Jeri Southern room ready for you by three."

After hanging up, Ella Rose stood motionless in her kitchen. The Christmas music continued to play, now a jazzy rendition of "Let It Snow" that felt oddly appropriate as she watched the flakes outside grow thicker.

She walked to her bedroom and slid open the bottom drawer of her dresser, pushing aside scarves until her fingers found the cool plastic of the Rusty Mic. She lifted it out, watching the light catch on the cheap gold paint.

"I must be crazy," she whispered. But as she placed the trophy on her dresser, out in the open for the first time in months, Ella Rose felt something stir within her. Not the sharp ache of recent grief, but something closer to curiosity, to possibility.

She crossed to her piano, running her fingers lightly over the keys where "A Single Spark" had been born. Perhaps this return to Bluestem would bring the closure she needed. Or perhaps it would simply be another gig, a chance to share her music in a beautiful setting.

Either way, she was going back. Back to the place where, for less than twenty-four hours in July, she'd glimpsed what it might feel like to fall in love.

Fifteen

ELLA ROSE

Ella Rose guided her Honda Civic down Main Street, the brick buildings of Bluestem now transformed by the magic of Christmas. Wreaths hung from lampposts, their red ribbons fluttering in the December breeze. White lights stretched between rooftops like a canopy of stars. The early winter darkness made the decorations pop against the night sky, so different from when she'd driven this route four months ago.

As the Whitemore Hotel came into view, Ella Rose's fingers tightened around the steering wheel. "Just another gig," she told herself. "Nothing more."

She parked, grabbed her overnight case and

guitar case from the back seat, and hurried toward the entrance, the cold air biting at her cheeks. Pine and holly garlands decorated each porch post, their scent cutting through the winter chill. A wreath adorned the front door, pine cones and red berries nestled among the greenery.

The moment she stepped inside, Ella Rose was enveloped in warmth, both from the crackling fire in the lobby fireplace and from the memories that washed over her. A magnificent Christmas tree stood in front of the lobby window, its branches heavy with ornaments and strings of popcorn and cranberries, its base surrounded by vintage toys and brightly wrapped packages.

"Ella!" LeAnne emerged from behind the desk, auburn hair in a neat bun with delicate silver snowflakes dangling from her ears. Her face lit up with genuine pleasure. "You made it!"

Ella Rose set down her cases and accepted LeAnne's warm embrace. "Thank you again for thinking of me for your Open House," she said, fighting the urge to scan the lobby for a tall, familiar figure.

"We're thrilled you could come on such short notice."

Ella followed, half-listening to LeAnne's cheerful chatter about the evening's expected attendance. The scent of cinnamon and cloves hung in the air, emanating from a pot of mulled cider warming on a sideboard.

"The Jeri Southern room is all ready for you," LeAnne said. She grabbed Ella Rose's overnight case and led the way up the grand staircase, now decorated with pine garlands interwoven with tiny white lights that cast a soft glow on the polished oak banister.

Fresh evergreen scented the second-floor hallway. When LeAnne unlocked the door, Ella stepped into a room both achingly familiar and newly festive. The navy bedspread now featured holiday pillows in red and green. On the writing desk sat a small tabletop Christmas tree decorated with miniature musical instruments: tiny pianos, violins, and a microphone ornament that tugged a reluctant smile from her.

LeAnne handed Ella Rose the key. "I'll be back in about thirty minutes to show you the ballroom setup."

"Wonderful. Thank you."

After LeAnne departed, Ella Rose unpacked her performance dress, a lush emerald green with a swing skirt. She hung it in the closet, smoothing a wrinkle from the fabric.

The window drew her like a magnet. Outside, the rose garden had transformed into snow-dusted bushes, neatly trimmed for winter. Looking down, she could almost hear his laugh, see the morning sun catching in his hair as he poured her another cup of coffee.

Her throat tightened. "Focus," she whispered, turning away from both the window and the memories it stirred. She busied herself arranging her makeup on the dresser, checking her set list one more time, anything to keep her mind occupied.

Thirty minutes later, LeAnne tapped on her door, and Ella Rose followed her downstairs to the ballroom. Twinkling lights criss-crossed the ceiling like stars. Pine garlands draped every windowsill, their fresh scent mixing with the sweetness from home-baked treats arranged on a buffet table. Round tables dotted the floor, each decorated with white poinsettias, gold stars, and delicate snow globes that caught and reflected the light.

"We've set up the stage over there," LeAnne said, gesturing to a small platform at the far end of the room.

Ella Rose walked onto the stage, testing its stability with a slight bounce. She hummed a few notes, listening to how they carried in the space. The acoustics were good. The room would amplify her voice without making it echo.

"This works perfectly," she said, surprised by how steady her voice sounded despite the butterflies in her stomach.

LeAnne smiled. "Wonderful! Guests start arriving at six-thirty. Your set begins at seven. Until then, your time is your own."

As LeAnne bustled away to continue her preparations, Ella Rose stood alone on the small stage. She closed her eyes, drawing in the pine-scented air, and imagined the empty ballroom filled with holiday revelers. In a few hours, she would stand here and sing, possibly with Sawyer in the audience. The thought sent a shiver through her that had nothing to do with the December chill.

She opened her eyes, squared her shoulders, and stepped down from the stage. It was time to prepare for the show.

Sixteen

SAWYER

Sawyer pushed open the doors of the Whitemore Hotel, his heart hammering against his ribs. He paused in the entryway, brushing snowflakes from his suit coat and stamping the snow from his boots.

The lobby was dressed for Christmas, the grand staircase wrapped in pine garlands dotted with red berries and tiny white lights. The familiar scent of cinnamon and cloves wafted from a pot of mulled cider warming on a table near the fireplace.

"Sawyer!" LeAnne emerged from behind the reception desk, and gave him a quick hug. "She's upstairs getting ready. She'll be down in a minute," she whispered. "The ballroom's pretty crowded, but I saved you a spot in the back, like you asked. I've just got a couple more things to attend to here, then I'll meet you in the ballroom and show you to your table."

Sawyer nodded. "Thanks, LeAnne. You're the best."

The ballroom doors stood open, revealing a space transformed. The ceiling was draped with strands of twinkling white lights that mimicked a starry sky, making him think of his walk with Rosie beneath the real stars that July night. Evergreen garlands framed each window, their piney scent mingling with the sweetness of white poinsettias arranged on each table. The room felt like winter magic distilled into physical form.

He stepped into the ballroom and froze. What was he thinking? Arranging for LeAnne to invite Rosie had seemed like a brilliant way to see her again, to explain his silence, to convince her that what they'd shared in July was real and worth pursuing. But now, with Rosie so close, doubt gnawed at him.

What if she didn't want to see him? What if she'd moved on? He had no right to expect otherwise, no right to assume she'd been holding on to what they'd shared as tightly as he had.

She's here, isn't she? he argued with himself. *That must mean something.*

LeAnne reappeared next to him. "Sorry to keep you waiting. Your table's this way."

"The room is beautiful, LeAnne," Sawyer said. "You've done an amazing job, as usual."

"Thank you. Decorating for the Open House is one of my favorite tasks of the whole year." She led him through the festive room to a table in the far corner marked Reserved. "You'll have a good view here, but you'll be out of her direct line of sight from the stage."

Sawyer nodded, unable to speak past the sudden tightness in his throat. This was really happening. In less than ten minutes, he would see Rosie again.

"Can I get you anything while you wait?" LeAnne asked. "Cider? Water? Eggnog?"

"I'm fine," Sawyer said, although "fine" was about the furthest thing from what he actually felt. His palms were damp, his collar suddenly too tight.

LeAnne squeezed his arm. "I need to mingle a bit before we start. Good luck, Sawyer." With that, she slipped away, leaving him alone at his table.

He pulled Rosie's note from his wallet. Its creases were sharp from countless readings. He unfolded it, his eyes finding the last lines:

Yours,

Ella Rose Tate (Rosie)

Sawyer settled into his chair. The room continued to fill. Families with children dressed in their holiday finest, elderly couples who had probably attended every Open House for decades, groups of friends laughing and chatting as they chose their seats.

Sawyer ignored them all. His attention was fixed solely on the doorway of the ballroom. Then, precisely at seven o'clock, she appeared. His Rosie.

Sawyer's breath caught in his throat. She wore an emerald green dress that caught the light as she moved, her guitar case slung over one shoulder. He'd imagined this moment a thousand times, rehearsed explanations, apologies, confessions. But now, seeing her again, his mind went blank, filled only with the fact that she was here. That she was back in Bluestem.

Sawyer leaned forward slightly, drinking in

the sight of her as LeAnne met her at the door and guided her through the ballroom toward the small stage.

A hush fell over the crowd as LeAnne tapped on the microphone. "Ladies and gentlemen, thank you all for coming to our Open House. We have a very special treat for you tonight, a wonderfully talented singer who's joining us from Lincoln, Nebraska. Please give a warm 'Bluestem Welcome' to Miss Ella Tate!"

Seventeen

ELLA ROSE

THE ROOM FELL silent the moment LeAnne's final note of introduction dissolved into the air. A single spotlight snapped on, bathing Ella Rose in a pool of warm light.

"Good evening," she said, her voice clear despite the flutter in her chest. "As LeAnne said, I'm Ella Tate, and I'm delighted to be here to celebrate Christmas with you."

The crowd applauded politely.

"I'd like to start with a classic that I think captures the spirit of the season." Her fingers found the opening chords of "Have Yourself a Merry Little Christmas," and she let the gentle melody fill the room. As she sang, her eyes scanned the crowd, an impulse she couldn't seem to control.

By the third song, a lively rendition of "Let It Snow", Ella Rose felt her shoulders relax. The crowd was warm and receptive, some singing along softly, others swaying to the rhythm. And there was no sign of the one face she both hoped and dreaded to see.

The realization brought a curious mixture of relief and disappointment, but Ella Rose channeled both into her performance, her voice growing stronger with each song.

Between her fifth and sixth songs, she paused to sip water, letting her gaze drift upward to where tiny lights glimmered against the dark ceiling. "I love what LeAnne has done with the decorations in this room. It's like performing under a winter sky."

The audience responded with appreciative murmurs and smiles. A woman near the front called out, "Your dress matches the tree perfectly!"

Ella Rose laughed. "It does, doesn't it!" she said, then launched into "Oh, Christmas Tree," inviting everyone to join in.

The room filled with voices, some pitch-perfect, others enthusiastically off-key, but all blending into a joyful communal sound that wrapped around Ella Rose like a warm embrace.

Ella Rose smiled. This was what she loved, creating moments where music connected people, where her voice could bring a room full of strangers into harmony.

Between songs, she shared small anecdotes: the origin of a carol, her grandmother's Christmas cookie traditions, her first time singing "Silent Night" in a church pageant. The crowd responded with knowing laughter and nods, drawn into the shared moments.

"This next song is my grandfather's favorite," she said, introducing "The Christmas Song." "He claims Nat King Cole sang it just for him every year."

As she sang, Ella Rose felt a sense of peace settle over her. Bluestem was just a town. A charming, memory-laden town, but still, just a place on a map. And this performance was just another in a long line of gigs that marked her career. Nothing more. Nothing less.

Her set list was nearly complete. Only "A Single Spark" remained. She'd debated whether to include it. But the song had taken on a life of its own these past few weeks, connecting with audiences in a way that surprised her. And maybe, she thought, singing it here, in Bluestem, would be a way to release the hopes and regrets she'd been carrying since July.

Ella Rose drew a deep breath, her fingers poised over the guitar strings. The crowd had fallen into an expectant hush, sensing the shift in energy. "This last piece is something I wrote a couple of months ago," she said, her voice softer now, more intimate. "It's about those moments that pass quickly but stay with us forever. The connections that might be brief but leave an imprint on our hearts."

She didn't mention that the song had been born in the darkness of her apartment after a date that had only made her miss Sawyer more. She didn't say that every word had emerged from the hollow space his silence had carved inside her. She simply began to play, the gentle opening notes of "A Single Spark" floating into the warm, pine-scented air of the Whitemore ballroom.

"A brief embrace of pure delight.
A memory etched in a starlit night.
I'm warmed by thoughts of what we shared.

And wonder if you know or care."

Ella Rose felt the familiar pain in her chest. Not as sharp now as it once had been, but still there. The faces in the audience blurred as she sank into the song, into its story of a starlit walk, karaoke, breakfast in a rose garden, and an unanswered goodbye note. Here, where it all began, she laid her heart bare.

Her voice strengthened as she moved into the chorus.

"Some fires burn a single time,
And then they're gone, but leave behind
A single spark, a quiet flame—
And nothing ever feels the same."

The second verse flowed from her like water, smooth and unstoppable. Ella Rose closed her eyes, no longer searching the crowd, no longer performing. This was something else. A release, perhaps, or a reckoning with the truth.

As she moved into the third verse, emotion colored her voice, giving it a slight rasp that only enhanced the raw honesty of the lyrics.

"If our paths should cross, some time, some how,
I'd risk it all, for you, right now.
Some hearts just know what's true and whole.
Mine calls your name, deep in my soul."

The ballroom was utterly still. Only her voice and guitar filled the silence. These strangers had become witnesses to something deeply personal, though they couldn't know the specific truth behind the words.

As she reached the bridge, her voice grew softer, almost a whisper, forcing the audience to lean in, to follow her into the heart of the song:

"I wouldn't ask to change the past,
Or beg the stars to make it last.
One perfect night, one perfect name—
And I'd still do it all the same."

And it was true, she realized. Despite the pain that had followed, despite the silence and the questions left unanswered, she wouldn't trade those few perfect hours in July. They had changed her: as a musician, as a person, as a woman capable of recognizing what she truly wanted.

The final chorus rose from somewhere deep within, powerful yet vulnerable, a perfect distillation of the journey she'd been on since leaving Bluestem four months ago:

"Some loves burn fast, but mark us deep,
And haunt our dreams when we go to sleep.
A single spark ignites a flame.

And nothing ever feels the same."

The last note hung in the air for a moment before gently fading away. Ella Rose kept her eyes closed, lingering in the emotional space of the song, saying a private goodbye to the hope she'd carried back to Bluestem with her.

When she finally opened her eyes, the applause was thunderous. Not the polite appreciation of earlier songs, but something more profound. Several people were on their feet. A woman in the front row dabbed at her eyes. LeAnne, near the refreshment table, clapped enthusiastically, a look of pride and something like satisfaction on her face.

"Thank you," Ella Rose said into the microphone, genuinely moved by the response. "You've been a wonderful audience. Merry Christmas to you all."

She stood to take a small bow, smiling as the applause continued. Her eyes swept across the room one last time, then froze as they reached the back of the ballroom.

Sawyer.

He stood along the back wall, tall and solid and unmistakably real. The noise of the crowd seemed to recede, the space between them contracting until it felt like they were the only two people in the room. Ella Rose's hands trembled slightly as she lowered her guitar, her mind racing. When had he arrived? How much of her song had he heard? Did he understand it was about him, about them?

He wore a dark blue suit and his hair was slightly tousled, as if he'd been running his fingers through it, that small nervous habit she'd found so endearing last summer. She couldn't read his expression from this distance, but his gaze was fixed on hers, open and intent.

He took a step forward, then hesitated, a flicker of uncertainty on his features. Ella Rose felt a rush of emotions—relief, surprise, disbelief—all tumbling over one another as she stared at him. She wanted to run to him, to demand an explanation for his silence, to tell him everything she'd been holding inside since July. Instead, she stood frozen on the stage, unsure of what to do next.

After four months of silence, after convincing herself that he hadn't cared enough to call, after writing a song to exorcise the ghost of what might have been, there he was, looking at her as if she were a mirage he couldn't quite believe in.

LeAnne stepped up to the stage, her smile wide as she took the microphone from Ella Rose's trembling hands. "Wasn't Ella wonderful, everyone?" The applause swelled again, but Ella Rose barely heard it over the rush of blood in her ears.

"But the fun isn't over yet," LeAnne continued. "Please join us in the sunroom, where a very special guest is waiting to hear your Christmas wishes!" She paused for effect, then added with a wink, "I hear he goes by the name Santa Claus!"

Eighteen

SAWYER

LAUGHTER AND CHATTER erupted as the crowd began to move, energized by the promise of more festivities and refreshments. Sawyer remained rooted, the crowd parting around him, his eyes fixed on Rosie. She remained on the stage, one hand still holding her guitar, the other gripping the microphone stand as if for support.

A woman in a red sweater stopped to talk to her, momentarily blocking Sawyer's view. He shifted, craning his neck to keep her in sight as more guests approached her. She responded to each one with a gracious smile and a quiet word, but her eyes kept finding his across the room, as if checking that he was still there, that he was real.

LeAnne appeared at his elbow. "Well?" she said. "Are you going to stand there all night, or are you going to talk to her?"

"I'm waiting for everyone to leave," Sawyer said, his voice low. "This isn't a conversation for an audience."

LeAnne nodded, understanding. "I'll take care of it." With gentle efficiency, LeAnne guided the last guests toward the exit, throwing one last encouraging glance over her shoulder at Sawyer as she pulled the ballroom doors closed behind her.

And then they were alone. Christmas music drifted from the speakers. Lights twinkled overhead, and pine garlands cast soft shadows. A mistletoe sprig, its white berries distinct, hung from the ceiling. Beyond the large windows, snowflakes fluttered down, dusting the outside in white.

It was beautiful, magical even, but Sawyer barely noticed. His entire focus remained on Rosie, on the way she finally set down her guitar with careful, deliberate movements, as if the instrument might shatter at any sudden motion.

Sawyer swallowed, his mouth dry. All the words he'd rehearsed, all the explanations he'd planned, all evaporated from his mind. There was only Rosie, looking at him with an expression he couldn't quite read. Surprise, yes, but also something deeper, more complex.

He wanted to cross the room, to climb the steps to the stage and pull her into his arms. He wanted to explain about the note, to apologize for the months of silence, to tell her how her song had reached into his chest and squeezed his heart until he could barely breathe.

The distance between them felt both impossible to cross and unbearable to maintain. Months of silence stretched between them like a physical thing. Months of wondering and regretting and missing. Months that would have been avoided if he'd just read her note that night.

Sawyer took a step, then another. Rosie's eyes widened slightly, but she didn't retreat. Instead, she seemed to stand a little straighter, her chin lifting in what might have been determination or defiance or simply an effort to maintain her composure.

He stopped, close enough to see the flecks of gold in her hazel eyes, close enough to catch the faint scent of her perfume.

"Hello, Rosie," he said.

Her voice was barely above a whisper, a blend of disbelief and something he dared to hope might be joy. "You're here."

"I'm here," he said, his own voice rough with emotion. "And I owe you an apology. A big one."

She looked down at him from the stage. "An apology? For what, exactly?" Her voice was soft but steady, betraying nothing of what she might be feeling.

"For messing everything up. For not reading your note until this past Monday." Sawyer pulled the folded note from his pocket, the paper soft and worn from repeated handling.

Ella Rose's eyes widened slightly, her gaze dropping to the note in his hand. "But I gave it to some folks in the kitchen. They said they'd make sure you got it."

"And they did." Sawyer stepped closer, resting one hand on the edge of the stage. "But I was in such a rush that day, helping Caleb with last-minute wedding stuff. I didn't know the note was from you. I thought it was contact information for a client. I shoved it into my pocket without looking at it, planning to read it later. And then I just forgot about it."

"The note was in your pocket? All this time?"

Sawyer nodded. "I thought you'd fled Bluestem when you had the chance," he said, the words he'd rehearsed finally finding their way out. "That maybe you wanted nothing to do with me, or that I'd somehow misread everything between us."

Rosie was silent for a long moment, the only sound the gentle strains of "I'll Be Home for Christmas" drifting through the speakers. Sawyer watched as a dozen emotions passed over her face—hurt, disbelief, frustration, then finally, relief.

"Four months," Rosie said, her voice catching. "Four months of thinking you'd read my note and decided not to call."

"I know." Sawyer's voice was low. "I can't get that time back. But I need you to know, I've missed you every day. Even when I thought you wanted nothing to do with me, I couldn't stop thinking about you."

"I missed you too," Rosie said, her voice barely above a whisper. "More than I wanted to admit, even to myself."

Sawyer extended his hand toward her. "Come down from there? Please?"

Rosie hesitated, then placed her hand in his.

As he helped her down the steps, he was struck by how right it felt to have her hand in his again, how perfectly their fingers fit together.

"I asked LeAnne to invite you to perform tonight. I didn't know if you'd accept, or if I'd have the courage to face you if you did."

Rosie smiled. "So you were the guest she mentioned? I wondered, but didn't dare hope."

Sawyer nodded. "I found your note on Monday. Called LeAnne that night. By Tuesday, she'd invited you to perform, and by Friday I was pacing my living room, wondering if I had any right to walk back into your life after all this time."

The Christmas music continued to play softly in the background, a slow, gentle melody filling the silence between them. Sawyer straightened his shoulders slightly. "I still owe you a dance," he said. "From the wedding. Remember?"

He gently placed his other hand at her waist, feeling the soft fabric of her dress beneath his fingers. Rosie's free hand rested on his shoulder. They moved together, finding the rhythm of the music as naturally as if they'd danced together a hundred times before.

The twinkling lights above cast a soft glow around them as they swayed across the empty ballroom floor. The pine scent of the garlands mixed with Rosie's perfume created a fragrance Sawyer knew he'd always associate with this moment, this second chance he'd never expected to have.

"I heard every word of your song," he said. "It was beautiful."

Rosie's eyes met his. "I wrote it after a date with someone else," she said. "All I could think about was you."

As they moved across the floor, Rosie sang along with the music, her voice a soft whisper between them. This private music performance just for him made his heart swell with emotion he couldn't have named if he'd tried.

Their dance carried them slowly around the ballroom, through pools of light and shadow. Soon, they stood beneath the mistletoe hanging from the ceiling, its white berries distinct on a red ribbon.

They both looked up, then at each other, a smile passing between them.

"Well," Sawyer said, "it is tradition."

Rosie's eyes sparkled as she looked up at him. "Far be it from me to break tradition."

Sawyer leaned down slowly, giving her every chance to pull away if this wasn't what she wanted. But she rose slightly on her toes to meet him halfway, her hand coming up to rest against his chest. Their lips met in a gentle kiss, sweet and full of promise.

When they parted, Sawyer kept her close, unwilling to let even an inch of unnecessary space between them. Four months had been distance enough.

"Do you want to go see Santa?" he asked. "I hear he takes Christmas wishes from grown-ups too."

Rosie shook her head, a smile playing on her lips. "I've already gotten my wish." She glanced toward the windows, where the snow fell in big, lazy flakes. "I was thinking the rose garden would look beautiful with snow on it. Want to see it with me?"

Sawyer felt his heart lift in a way it hadn't in months. Years, maybe. "I'd love to."

He led her toward the French doors that opened onto the garden, where the snow-covered rose bushes waited like old friends, and the light from the ballroom spilled out onto the path, lending a warm glow to the winter night.

As they stepped outside into the winter night, Rosie tucked herself against his side, her head finding its place on his shoulder.

And Sawyer knew, with a certainty that filled his entire being, that the spark they'd found in the summer had never really gone out. It had simply been waiting, like the stars, for the right moment to reappear.

Epilogue

ELLA ROSE

Sawyer's truck rumbled to a stop in the gravel lot of the Rusty Spur. The opening notes of "A Single Spark" began to play on the radio. "Hold on," Sawyer said, a grin spreading across his face. "We need to hear this." From the back seat, Amber leaned forward between the headrests while Caleb nodded, giving Sawyer a thumb's up.

Ella gasped, her hand flying to her mouth. "That's me! That's my song on the radio!" She cranked up the volume, her heart hammering against her ribs. The sound of her own voice filled the truck cab, the melody she'd crafted in the darkest hours of that lonely night now soaring through the airwaves.

"I know," Sawyer said, his grin widening as he watched her reaction. "I heard it yesterday on my way to a job site. Called the station right away to find out when they'd play it again. The DJ said it's been getting requests all week." He reached over and took her hand, his thumb tracing circles over her knuckles. "You did it, Rosie."

Ella Rose turned to face him, her eyes shining with unshed tears. The irony wasn't lost on her—the song born from heartbreak over Sawyer was now playing while she sat beside him in his truck, their fingers intertwined.

As the final notes faded and the DJ's voice returned to announce the next song, Ella Rose felt a rush of emotions she couldn't quite name. Pride, certainly—hearing her music on the radio was a dream she'd carried since childhood. But there was something bittersweet about it too— the knowledge that her greatest creative triumph had been born from the pain of losing him.

"What are you thinking about right now?" Sawyer asked.

"Just thinking about the first time we were

here. Two strangers, just sharing a meal together," she said, and gave his fingers a gentle squeeze. "Funny how things work out, isn't it?"

Sawyer's smile deepened, crinkling the corners of his eyes in that way that still made her heart skip. "Best decision I ever made."

From the back seat, Caleb cleared his throat dramatically. "Skipping our rehearsal dinner to hang out with a complete stranger? I'd have to question that logic."

"Ignore him," Amber said, leaning forward between the seats. "He's just jealous because your love story has its own soundtrack."

Ella Rose laughed as they climbed out of the truck. A gentle breeze ruffled her hair as Sawyer's arm slipped around her waist, pulling her close against his side as they walked toward the entrance.

The bar was lively for a Friday night, with locals crowded around tables and pressed against the worn wooden bar. The karaoke setup was already in place, the small stage area cleared at the far end of the room. Familiar country music played over the speakers, not loud enough to drown conversation but just enough to create a blanket of sound that wrapped around the patrons.

"Well, if it isn't the Jennings crew, plus one!" Wyatt said, from behind the bar. "I was hoping you'd all make an appearance." He set down the glass he was drying and made his way around the bar toward them. "Any chance we're going to hear another duet tonight?"

"Not a chance," said Sawyer.

"What about you two?" he asked, looking at Caleb and Amber.

Caleb grimaced and shook his head. "I love my wife, but our musical talents are best kept private."

"He's not wrong," Amber said, smiling. "I think we'll leave the singing to the professionals tonight."

"Looks like I'm flying solo," Ella Rose said, leaning into Sawyer's side.

"That's okay with me," Wyatt said. "Any night that Ella Tate graces our stage is a good night for the Rusty Spur!"

Ella Rose laughed. "A girl could get used to that kind of flattery," she said.

"So, what brings you in tonight?" Wyatt asked. "Other than my mom's apple pie."

"We're here to celebrate Amber and Caleb's one year wedding anniversary, and what better place to do it than here, where Sawyer and I had our first date."

"A wedding anniversary and a first date?" Wyatt said, shaking his head in amusement. "You know there's such a thing as too much romance, right?"

Sawyer let out a lighthearted laugh, and Ella Rose felt that same familiar flutter. "We'll take our chances."

Wyatt turned to Amber and Caleb, his broad smile easy and genuine. "A year already? Seems like it was just yesterday that Caleb was nearly passing out at the altar."

"I was not passing out," Caleb said, although his cheeks reddened slightly. "It was just really hot in that suit."

"I'll second that," said Sawyer.

"Right, the heat," Wyatt said, with a knowing wink. "Anyway, first round's on the house for the anniversary couple."

"In that case," Amber said, "I'll have a glass of that wine I liked last time. The red one."

"Just some sweet tea for me," said Rosie.

"Coming right up." Wyatt nodded. "And for you gentlemen?"

"Beer for me," Caleb said.

"Same," Sawyer added.

Wyatt was just handing them their drinks when Rosie saw a familiar face weaving her way through the crowd. Hannah, the woman she'd left her note with at the wedding, approached the bar, navigating between the bustling tables. Her cheeks were pink, either from the warmth of the room or the excitement of the night, and she grinned as she waved.

"Hey, Rosie!" she said, sliding up beside them. "Sorry to interrupt, but I wanted to introduce Rosie to someone."

"Rosie? I thought you were racing through the crowd to get to me!" Wyatt said.

Hannah rolled her eyes at Wyatt's teasing. "You, I can see anytime! Right now, I have some important newspaper business to take care of."

Hannah gestured toward the dark-haired woman following behind her. "Rosie, this is Alyssa. She's the new journalist at the Gazette. Alyssa, this is the singer Ella Tate."

"Hello, Ella. I've heard so much about you. I'm thrilled to finally meet you." Alyssa extended her hand. "I'd love to do a feature about your singing and writing career. Would you be open to an interview?"

Before Ella Rose could answer, Sawyer gently clapped Caleb on the back and steered him away from the bar. "That's our signal. Let's go find a table while these two hash out the details. See you in a bit, Rosie."

Ella Rose turned her full attention back to Alyssa. "I'd love to do an interview," she said, surprised by the request. "That's very flattering."

"Great!" Alyssa pulled out a slim notebook and jotted a quick note. "I'll call you on Monday."

As soon as Alyssa and Hannah disappeared into the crowd, Ella Rose waved to Wyatt, who was pouring a drink at the end of the bar. He nodded and walked down to her.

"All set for later?" she asked quietly, glancing over her shoulder to make sure Sawyer wasn't watching.

"You bet," Wyatt said. "I've got you scheduled for the third slot, just like you asked. And your song's already cued up in the system."

"Thanks, Wyatt. This means a lot to me."

"Are you kidding? I wouldn't miss this for the

world." Wyatt nodded toward their table, where Sawyer was laughing at something Caleb had said. "He has no idea, does he?"

"None whatsoever," Ella Rose said, unable to keep the smile from her face. "He thinks I'm singing 'Crazy' again."

Wyatt grinned. "Well, your secret's safe with me. And I'm pretty sure he's going to love it."

Ella Rose felt a flutter of nervous excitement in her stomach. She'd been working on this song for weeks, polishing every note and lyric until it perfectly captured what she wanted to say.

"I should get back before they start wondering where I am," she said, glancing back at their table.

"Break a leg," Wyatt said with a wink. "Or should I say, melt his heart."

Ella Rose laughed as she turned away from the bar, her steps light despite the nervous anticipation building in her chest. As she made her way to their table, she caught Sawyer's eye across the room. He smiled that smile, the one that seemed reserved just for her, and she knew, without a shadow of a doubt, that this song, this night, was exactly what she wanted to give him.

"Everything okay?" he asked, his eyes searching hers.

Ella Rose nodded. "Everything's perfect."

Wyatt stepped up to the microphone, tapping it twice with his finger. The feedback echoed through the Rusty Spur, and conversations hushed as he cleared his throat. "All right, folks," he said, his voice carrying easily through the now-crowded bar. "It's that time of the week again. Karaoke night at the Rusty Spur is officially underway!"

A cheer rose from the tables, and Ella Rose felt a flutter of nerves in her stomach as she glanced at the small stage where, in just a short while, she would be performing her newest song.

"First up, we have Tom with 'Friends in Low Places'!" The opening notes of Garth Brooks' classic filled the room, and the middle-aged man on the stage launched into a surprisingly strong rendition that had most of the bar singing along by the chorus.

Ella Rose joined in automatically, the familiar lyrics providing a welcome distraction from the butterflies in her stomach. She felt Sawyer's voice rumbling beside her as he sang too, his arm still draped comfortably around her shoulders.

The man finished to enthusiastic applause, taking an exaggerated bow before handing the microphone back to Wyatt. "Let's hear it one more time for Tom!" Wyatt said, clapping along with the crowd.

"Next up, we have Joe with 'Sweet Caroline'!"

Ella Rose's heart began to pound harder. After this song, it would be her turn. She reached for her tea, trying to steady her hands, which had begun to tremble slightly.

Sawyer noticed immediately. "Are you okay?" he asked, his voice low with concern. "You seem nervous."

"I'm fine," Ella Rose said, though she knew her voice lacked conviction. "I just ... I want to make you proud," she said, squeezing his hand.

His expression softened. "You always do."

Across the table, Amber caught Ella Rose's eye and gave her a subtle thumbs-up. Ella Rose had told her about her planned surprise for Sawyer last week. Amber's enthusiasm had been exactly the encouragement she'd needed.

"And next up," Wyatt's voice cut through her

thoughts, "we've got a special treat for you all. Please welcome back to the Rusty Spur stage, Miss Ella Tate!"

A round of applause rippled through the bar. "Go show 'em how it's done," Sawyer said with a proud smile.

Ella Rose leaned over and pressed a quick kiss to his cheek, her lips lingering near his ear. "This one's for you," she whispered before sliding out of the booth.

Her legs felt unsteady as she made her way to the stage, weaving between tables where patrons nodded and smiled in recognition. She'd become something of a local favorite during her weekend visits over the past seven months, always singing a song or two when they came to the Rusty Spur.

But tonight was different. Tonight wasn't about entertaining strangers. It was about the man watching her from their corner table, the one whose smile had changed her life forever.

As she stepped onto the small stage, the bar grew quieter. Wyatt handed her the microphone with a wink, then moved to the karaoke setup where her special track was cued and waiting.

Ella Rose took a deep breath and looked

straight at Sawyer. He was watching her with that look of pride and affection that never failed to warm her from the inside out. Caleb nudged him with an elbow, saying something that made Sawyer laugh without taking his eyes off her.

The bar fell silent as she lifted the microphone to her lips. Her heart pounded so loudly she was sure the microphone would pick it up.

"Thank you all," she began, her voice steadier than she felt. "Tonight, I'm not going to sing someone else's song. Instead, I'm going to sing one of my own. It's called 'My Way to You.'" She paused and took a deep breath. "And I'm dedicating it to Sawyer Jennings, the man who taught me that sometimes, ending up in the wrong spot, is the only way to find exactly where you're meant to be."

A collective "aww" rose from the crowd. From their table, Amber nudged Caleb, both of them grinning widely. Ella Rose looked at Sawyer, whose expression had transformed from proud encouragement to stunned surprise. His lips parted slightly, his eyes widening as he realized what was happening.

This wasn't just another karaoke performance. This was her heart, set to music, offered to him in front of the entire town where their story had begun.

Ella Rose nodded to Wyatt, and as the first gentle notes of her melody began to play, she saw Caleb lean over to whisper something in Sawyer's ear. Amber was already reaching for her phone, clearly planning to record the moment.

But Sawyer didn't respond to either of them. He sat perfectly still, his eyes never leaving Ella Rose's face, a look of wonder and anticipation washing over his features as he waited for her to begin.

The first notes of the melody filled the Rusty Spur, her voice clear and strong despite the emotion swelling in her chest.

I traveled to the wrong small town,
And through the wrong front door.
But in a place I shouldn't be,
I found myself, and more.

The bar had fallen completely silent. Even the usual clink of glasses had stopped as everyone listened, captivated by the raw emotion in her voice. Ella Rose watched Amber wipe a tear, her phone capturing the moment.

Her voice grew stronger as she moved into the second verse.

One duet on a Friday night,
Our pathway lit with stars.
And ever since that magic night,
My heart is where you are.

The lyrics carried her back to their walk beneath the Bluestem sky, to their first kiss, to every moment that had led them here. The music flowed through her, each note carrying pieces of their story: the misunderstanding that had separated them, the Christmas miracle that had brought them back together, and every weekend since, building a life between two towns, between hello and goodbye.

As she reached the third verse, her voice softened with emotion.

Some call it fate, some call it chance,
This love I can't ignore.
The stars looked down and smiled that night,
When I walked through that door.

She saw Sawyer swallow hard, his eyes never leaving hers, and she poured every ounce of love she felt for him into the words.

The instrumental interlude gave her a moment to breathe, to steady herself for the bridge. The bar remained hushed, dozens of people holding their breath with her, witnesses to something rare and precious unfolding before them.

When she began the bridge, her voice took on a new depth, rich with the certainty she felt in her heart.

From strangers to forever,
In just one starry night.
Two hearts had found each other,
And everything seemed right.

The words hung in the air between them, a promise and a question all at once.

Sawyer's eyes glistened in the dim light of the bar, and Ella Rose felt her own vision blur with unshed tears as she moved into the final verse, her voice growing stronger with each word.

Our journey wasn't easy,
We made mistakes, that's true.
But I'd take that wrong turn every time
To find my way to you.

As the last note faded into silence, the Rusty Spur erupted in applause. Someone in the back let out a whistle, and several people rose to their feet.

But Ella Rose barely registered any of it. She stood on the small stage, her heart pounding in her chest, feeling more exposed and more certain than she ever had in her life.

She'd done it. She'd put every feeling, every hope, every dream she had for their future into those lyrics, and now they hung in the air between them, impossible to take back.

For a moment, she couldn't move, caught in the intensity of Sawyer's gaze across the room. Then she saw him rise from his seat. The crowd's applause faded as Sawyer made his way toward the stage, his steps purposeful. A murmur rippled through the bar as people noticed his approach, the atmosphere shifting from appreciation to anticipation.

He reached the edge of the small stage and paused, looking up at her with such undisguised love that it took her breath away. Then, to her surprise, he stepped up onto the platform beside her.

A hush fell over the room once more. In her peripheral vision, Ella Rose could see Amber gripping Caleb's arm, her phone still recording, her expression a mixture of excitement and barely contained emotion.

"Can I borrow this for a second?" Sawyer asked, gesturing to the microphone.

Ella Rose nodded, unable to form words, and handed it to him. Their fingers brushed in the exchange, and even that small contact sent a current of electricity up her arm.

Sawyer cleared his throat, his eyes never leaving hers even as he addressed the crowded bar. "So, I had a plan," he said, his voice warm and slightly rough with emotion. "I was going to take Rosie to the Whitemore's rose garden tomorrow morning. I had it all arranged with LeAnne—breakfast under the arbor where we had our first real date, roses everywhere."

A soft murmur rippled through the crowd, and Ella Rose's hand flew to her mouth as she understood what was happening.

Sawyer reached into his pocket and pulled out a small velvet box. The sight of it sent a jolt through Ella Rose's entire body. The crowd let out a collective gasp as he slowly, deliberately, lowered himself to one knee before her.

"But then you sang that song," he said, his voice catching slightly, "and I realized there's no more perfect place than right here, right now, where our story began."

Tears blurred Ella Rose's vision as Sawyer opened the box to reveal a delicate ring with a single diamond that caught the stage lights and scattered them like stars.

"Ella Rose Tate," he said, his voice steady now, filled with certainty, "you walked into the wrong town and the wrong hotel that day, and straight into my heart."

He took a breath, his eyes never leaving hers. "You sang about finding your way to me, but the truth is, I think we found our way to each other. And I don't want to spend another day without you. I want forever, Rosie. Will you marry me?"

The room collectively held its breath. Ella Rose felt tears spill onto her cheeks as joy, pure and overwhelming, flooded through her. She dropped to her knees in front of him, bringing them face to face, and cupped his cheeks in her trembling hands.

"Yes," she whispered, the single word carrying all the certainty in her heart. Then louder, so everyone could hear, "Yes!"

The Rusty Spur erupted in cheers and applause as Sawyer slid the ring onto her finger, his own hand trembling slightly. Then his arms were around her, lifting her to her feet as his lips found hers in a kiss that tasted of joy and promise and forever.

When they finally broke apart, breathless and laughing, the crowd was on its feet. Ella Rose could see Amber wiping tears from her cheeks while still trying to hold her phone steady. Caleb was clapping and whistling, his face split in a wide grin.

Wyatt's voice boomed over the microphone he'd reclaimed. "I think we can all agree we have our karaoke champions for tonight!" he announced, reaching under the bar and producing the familiar gold plastic trophy. "And the next round is on the house! To Rosie and Sawyer!"

"To Rosie and Sawyer!" the crowd echoed, raising their glasses.

Sawyer's arm wrapped securely around her waist as they stepped down from the stage, accepting congratulations and well-wishes from what seemed like the entire population of Bluestem. Caleb pulled his brother into a bear hug while Amber threw her arms around Ella Rose.

"So," he said, his lips close to her ear as the celebration continued around them, "what do you think about getting married in the Whitemore Rose Garden? Under those stars you love so much?"

Ella Rose looked up at him, at the face that had become home to her. "I think," she said, rising on her tiptoes to brush her lips against his, "that sounds like the perfect place to start our forever."

Continue your journey to Bluestem with ...

FALLING FOR THE RODEO COWBOY

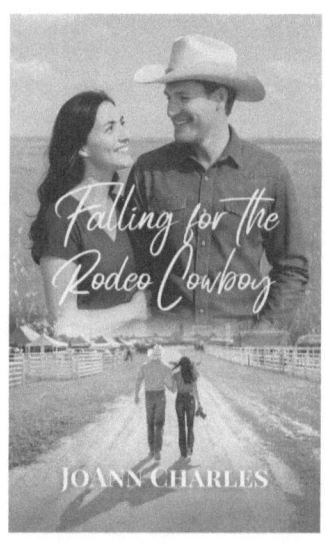

When Chicago journalist Alyssa Downing arrives in Bluestem, hoping to escape her grief, the last thing she expects is to stumble—literally—into rodeo cowboy Riley Manchester. Her first brush with the hometown cowboy is anything but graceful, but through her camera lens she begins to see the grit, determination, and heart beneath his cowboy swagger.

Riley has his hands full—splitting time

CONTINUE YOUR JOURNEY TO BLUESTEM WITH

between the rodeo circuit and his family's business. The last thing he needs is a big-city journalist turning his world upside down. But Bluestem has a way of rewriting stories ... and sometimes even healing hearts.

Loved your journey to Bluestem?

If you enjoyed your visit to Bluestem and **Wrong Wedding Right Guy** touched your heart, please take a moment to leave a short review.

Your review helps other readers discover these clean, heartwarming stories and keeps the Bluestem series growing.

LOVED YOUR JOURNEY TO BLUESTEM?

Even a few words make a big difference.

Join JoAnn's Dream Team at joanncharles.substack.com and be the first to know when one of her ebook novellas is free on Amazon!

About the Author

JoAnn Charles writes clean, heartwarming romantic stories filled with small-town charm, hope, and happily-ever-afters. Her Bluestem cozy novels celebrate love, laughter, and the power of community, set in a place where everyone knows your name and second chances are always on the menu at Daisy's Diner.

When she's not writing about love in Bluestem, Jo can be found enjoying coffee with friends, dreaming up her next story, or spending time with her family.

She also writes children's books under the pen name **N. L. Sharp**.

www.ingramcontent.com/pod-product-compliance
Lightning Source LLC
LaVergne TN
LVHW040145080526
838202LV00042B/3031